ANIMAL FARM

George Orwell

COLLINS
CLASSICS

William Collins
An imprint of HarperCollins*Publishers*
1 London Bridge Street
London SE1 9GF

WilliamCollinsBooks.com

HarperCollins*Publishers*
1st Floor, Watermarque Building, Ringsend Road
Dublin 4, Ireland

This William Collins paperback edition published in Great Britain in 2021

7

A catalogue record for this book
is available from the British Library

ISBN 978-0-00-832205-2; 978-0-00-844263-7

Life & Times section © HarperCollins*Publishers* Ltd
Fran Fabriczki asserts her moral right as the author of the Life & Times section
Classic Literature: Words and Phrases adapted from
Collins English Dictionary

Typesetting in Kalix by Palimpsest Book Production Limited,
Falkirk, Stirlingshire

Printed and bound in the UK using 100% renewable electricity at CPI Group (UK) Ltd

MIX
Paper from
responsible sources
FSC™ C007454

This book is produced from independently certified FSC™ paper
to ensure responsible forest management.

For more information visit: www.harpercollins.co.uk/green

History of William Collins

In 1819, millworker William Collins from Glasgow, Scotland, set up a company for printing and publishing pamphlets, sermons, hymn books, and prayer books. That company was Collins and was to mark the birth of HarperCollins Publishers as we know it today. The long tradition of Collins dictionary publishing can be traced back to the first dictionary William co-published in 1825, *Greek and English Lexicon*. Indeed, from 1840 onwards, he began to produce illustrated dictionaries and even obtained a licence to print and publish the Bible.

Soon after, William published the first Collins novel; however, it was the time of the Long Depression, where harvests were poor, prices were high, potato crops had failed, and violence was erupting in Europe. As a result, many factories across the country were forced to close down and William chose to retire in 1846, partly due to the hardships he was facing.

Aged 30, William's son, William II, took over the business. A keen humanitarian with a warm heart and a generous spirit, William II was truly 'Victorian' in his outlook. He introduced new, up-to-date steam presses and published affordable editions of Shakespeare's works and *The Pilgrim's Progress*, making them available to the masses for the first time.

A new demand for educational books meant that success came with the publication of travel books, scientific books, encyclopedias, and dictionaries. This demand to be educated led to the later publication of atlases, and Collins also held the monopoly on scripture writing at the time.

In the 1860s Collins began to expand and diversify and the idea of 'books for the millions' was developed, although the phrase wasn't coined until 1907. Affordable editions of classical literature were published, and in 1903 Collins introduced 10 titles in their Collins Handy Illustrated Pocket Novels. These proved so popular that a few years later this had increased to an output of 50 volumes, selling nearly half a million in their year of publication. In the same year, The Everyman's Library was also instituted, with the idea of publishing an affordable library of the most important classical works, biographies, religious and philosophical treatments, plays, poems, travel, and adventure. This series eclipsed all competition at the time, and the introduction of paperback books in the 1950s helped to open that market and marked a high point in the industry.

HarperCollins is and has always been a champion of the classics, and the current Collins Classics series follows in this tradition – publishing classical literature that is affordable and available to all. Beautifully packaged, highly collectible, and intended to be reread and enjoyed at every opportunity.

Life & Times

'What I have most wanted to do [...] is to make political writing into an art' George Orwell claimed in his 1946 essay 'Why I Write'. Never has such a clearly stated literary manifesto been realised so completely. Achieving moderate success for much of his career, George Orwell's final two novels, *Animal Farm* and *Nineteen Eighty-Four*, swiftly elevated him to the upper echelons of the literary firmament, with his combination of uniquely straightforward prose and deeply political content. The road leading to these two great pieces of political art was, unsurprisingly, paved with years of intense political engagement, in the turbulent decades of the early twentieth century.

Early years

George Orwell was born Eric Arthur Blair in India in 1903 to Ida Limouzin, a woman of French descent, and Richard Walmsley Blair, a British agent in the Opium Department of the Indian Civil Service. As an infant, he moved back to England with his mother and sister, where he would spend his early childhood among his female relations in the rural surroundings of the Oxfordshire countryside.

He attended St Cyprian's School, which he despised (for the harsh treatment he received there and its abundance of rich, privileged young children), and later Eton, where he found his persona as the rebellious 'under-privileged' scholarship student worked in his favour. Academically, he did not do well at Eton, though he read voraciously. Among his early literary influences were H.G. Wells, George Bernard Shaw, Jack London and Rudyard Kipling. Renowned dystopian author Aldous Huxley – whose work would often be compared to his own in later years – briefly taught him French at Eton. The First World War took place during his time there, leading to an early engagement with world politics that would influence his later views.

Having neglected his studies at Eton, the traditional route of an Oxbridge education was barred for Orwell, and he decided to join the Indian Civil Service upon leaving in 1921. He would later describe the years he spent in Burma as a policeman in the Indian Imperial Police as 'the wasted years', although they were crucial in providing him inspiration for much of his writing, as well as providing motivation to succeed as an author, as opposed to spending his life in public service. His time spent as an enforcer of Britain's imperial rule also sparked his lifelong uneasiness with authority – a factor that played an important role in his decision to move back to England and make a career out of writing.

'Down and Out' years

Although – to his family's dismay – Orwell made clear his writing ambitions upon leaving India, it would be many years before he succeeded in breaking into the literary world. He spent the intervening years honing his craft and gaining life experience in the slums of London, and later Paris. He drew inspiration from his acute study of daily life to draw out larger issues that plagued society; these series of observations would later become the basis for *Down and Out in Paris and London* (published in 1933).

Returning to England Orwell turned his attention to writing fiction, struggling to adapt his clear, journalistic prose style to novels. The novels he wrote during this time include *Burmese Days* and *A Clergyman's Daughter*. As he would later claim, they were attempts at 'enormous naturalistic novels with unhappy endings', which is what he had been accustomed to reading as a boy growing up in the Edwardian era.

During this time, he worked several odd jobs to stay afloat, among them positions as a teacher and a bookseller, all the time continuing to write for various publications, and working on his own projects. In 1936, his publisher, Victor Gollancz, asked him to work on a project uniquely suited to his talents: documenting the areas of Northern England most affected by the Depression. He immersed himself in the life of the destitute and his observations culminated in the publication of *The Road to Wigan Pier* – the first book to bring him substantial critical acclaim.

The Spanish Civil War

On the cusp of literary success Orwell decided to travel to Spain, and, like many of his contemporaries – including American writers John Dos Passos and Ernest Hemingway – take part in the bloody Spanish Civil War. His generation of artists and intellectuals followed the events of the Civil War closely, and it became the battleground for political philosophy as much as physical warfare. Orwell's commitment to fighting fascism in Spain came under scrutiny, as the various factions of the political left were pitted against each other, which left him feeling that the socialist revolution had been betrayed.

Returning from the war, he became vocally critical of the Stalinist regime, equating their totalitarianism with that of the fascists across Europe. Left-wing publications that had previously embraced him refused to publish his essays, and his account of the Spanish Civil War, *Homage to Catalonia*, was refused by his editor Gollancz, eventually going to a smaller publishing house, Secker & Warburg.

Having suffered a near-fatal injury in Spain, Orwell's health continued to deteriorate, and he spent half a year in Morocco recovering, completing his novel *Coming Up for Air* during his time there.

The Second World War

Despite his disillusionment both with his own country's capitalism and the state of left-wing politics, when the Second World War began Orwell was desperate to fight for his country. This revealed his unique blend of anti-capitalist yet patriotic politics, and his belief that the war could lead to a revolution that united working and middle classes. His thoughts on the topic were explored in his critically acclaimed book, *The Lion and the Unicorn*. He served in the Home Guard for three years during the war, continued to write numerous essays and reviews for various publications, and later took a job in broadcasting with the BBC, during which time he began his work on *Animal Farm*.

Animal Farm

All animals are equal, but some animals are more equal than others.

It is with such characteristically caustic use of language that Orwell wrote his world-famous fable of the Russian Revolution. All the major players of the historical event have their animal counterpart: the pigs as the leaders of the revolution (Old Major as Lenin and Napoleon as Stalin); the young pups reared to be vicious executors of their will as a stand-in for the Russian secret service; Boxer the horse as the exploited and overworked working class; and even Orwell himself is thought to appear in the form of the cynical but clear-headed donkey, Benjamin. With his anthropomorphic ensemble of animals, Orwell fused biting political critique with humour and wit, resulting in an enjoyable and educational read that continues to thrill readers of every age to this day.

The initial success of *Animal Farm* is often considered the result of mounting tensions leading up to the Cold War – however, Orwell was prescient rather than reactionary in his criticism of the Stalinist regime. He wrote *Animal Farm* at a time when England was in a strong and public alliance with Stalinist Russia, and Orwell therefore had difficulty finding a publisher for his novel, despite having a prolific and acclaimed literary output to back him up. In later years, it transpired that a Soviet spy working in the Ministry of Information had pressured several publishers to reject Orwell's manuscript – testimony to the power of Orwell's words. After it finally found a home with Secker & Warburg, it was published in 1945, at the end of the war, to enormous critical and commercial success, first in England, and later on, even more so, in America.

It would have been difficult to imagine that Orwell could surpass the success of *Animal Farm*, but he did so with the publication of his final novel, *Nineteen Eighty-Four*, in which he imagines a future totalitarian regime, rather than offering a thinly veiled critique of an existing one. Unfortunately, due to his long-standing health problems, Orwell could only fleetingly enjoy his literary success and financial comfort – he died on January 21, 1950 at the age of forty-six.

CONTENTS

ANIMAL FARM

CHAPTER 1

Mr. Jones, of the Manor Farm, had locked the hen-houses for the night, but was too drunk to remember to shut the pop-holes. With the ring of light from his lantern dancing from side to side he lurched across the yard, kicked off his boots at the back door, drew himself a last glass of beer from the barrel in the scullery, and made his way up to bed, where Mrs. Jones was already snoring.

As soon as the light in the bedroom went out there was a stirring and a fluttering all through the farm buildings. Word had gone round during the day that old Major, the prize Middle White boar, had had a strange dream on the previous night and wished to communicate it to the other animals. It had been agreed that they should all meet in the big barn as soon as Mr. Jones was safely out of the way. Old Major (so he was always called, though the name under which he had been exhibited was Willingdon Beauty) was so highly regarded on the farm that everyone was quite ready to lose an hour's sleep in order to hear what he had to say.

At one end of the big barn, on a sort of raised platform, Major was already ensconced on his bed of straw, under a lantern which hung from a beam. He was twelve years old and had lately grown rather stout, but he was still a majestic-looking pig, with a wise and benevolent appearance in spite of the fact that his tushes had never been cut. Before long the other animals began to arrive and make themselves comfortable after their different fashions. First came the three dogs, Bluebell, Jessie, and Pincher, and then the pigs, who settled down in the straw immediately in front of the platform. The hens perched themselves on the window sills, the pigeons fluttered up to the rafters, the sheep and cows lay down behind the pigs and began to chew the cud. The two cart-horses, Boxer and Clover, came in together, walking very slowly and setting down their vast hairy hoofs with great care lest there should be some small animal concealed in the straw. Clover was a stout motherly mare approaching middle life, who had never quite got her figure back after her fourth foal. Boxer was an enormous beast, nearly eighteen hands high, and as strong as any two ordinary horses put together. A white stripe down his nose gave him a somewhat stupid appearance, and in fact he was not of first-rate intelligence, but he was universally respected for his steadiness of character and tremendous powers of work. After the horses came Muriel, the white goat, and Benjamin, the donkey. Benjamin was the oldest animal on the farm, and the worst tempered. He seldom talked, and when he did, it was usually to make some cynical remark—for instance, he would say that God had given him a tail to keep the flies off, but that he would sooner have had no tail and no flies. Alone among the animals on the farm he never laughed. If asked why, he would say that he saw nothing to laugh at. Nevertheless, without openly admitting it, he was devoted to Boxer; the two of them usually spent their Sundays together in the small paddock beyond the orchard, grazing side by side and never speaking.

The two horses had just lain down when a brood of ducklings which had lost their mother, filed into the barn, cheeping feebly and wandering from side to side to find some place where they would not be trodden on. Clover made a sort of wall round them with her great foreleg, and the ducklings nestled down inside it and promptly fell asleep. At the last moment Mollie, the foolish, pretty white mare who drew Mr. Jones's trap, came mincing daintily in, chewing at a lump of sugar. She took a place near the front and began flirting her white mane, hoping to draw attention to the red ribbons it was plaited with. Last of all came the cat, who looked round, as usual, for the warmest place, and finally squeezed herself in between Boxer and Clover; there she purred contentedly throughout Major's speech without listening to a word of what he was saying.

All the animals were now present except Moses, the tame raven, who slept on a perch behind the back door. When Major saw that they had all made themselves comfortable and were waiting attentively, he cleared his throat and began:

"Comrades, you have heard already about the strange dream that I had last night. But I will come to the dream later. I have something else to say first. I do not think, comrades, that I shall be with you for many months longer, and before I die, I feel it my duty to pass on to you such wisdom as I have acquired. I have had a long life, I have had much time for thought as I lay alone in my stall, and I think I may say that I understand the nature of life on this earth as well as any animal now living. It is about this that I wish to speak to you.

"Now, comrades, what is the nature of this life of ours? Let us face it: our lives are miserable, laborious, and short. We are born, we are given just so much food as will keep the breath in our bodies, and those of us who are capable of it are forced to work to the last atom of our strength; and the very instant that our usefulness has come to an end we are slaughtered with hideous cruelty. No animal in England knows the meaning of happiness or leisure after he is a year old. No animal in England is free. The life of an animal is misery and slavery: that is the plain truth.

"But is this simply part of the order of Nature? Is it because this land of ours is so poor that it cannot afford a decent life to those who dwell upon it? No, comrades, a thousand times no! The soil of England is fertile, its climate is good, it is capable of affording food in abundance to an enormously greater number of animals than now inhabit it. This single farm of ours would support a dozen horses, twenty cows, hundreds of sheep—and all of them living in a comfort and a dignity that are now almost beyond our imagining. Why then do we continue in this miserable condition? Because nearly the whole of the produce of our labour is stolen from us by human beings. There, comrades, is the answer to all our problems. It is summed up in a single word—Man. Man is the only real enemy we have. Remove Man from the scene, and the root cause of hunger and overwork is abolished for ever.

"Man is the only creature that consumes without producing. He does not give milk, he does not lay eggs, he is too weak to pull the plough, he cannot run fast enough to catch rabbits. Yet he is lord of all the animals. He sets them to work, he gives back to them the bare minimum that will prevent them from starving, and the rest he keeps for himself. Our labour tills the soil, our dung fertilises it, and yet there is not one of us that owns more than his bare skin. You cows that I see before me, how many thousands of gallons of milk have you given during this last year? And what has happened to that milk which should have been breeding up sturdy calves? Every drop of it has gone down the throats of our enemies. And you hens, how many eggs have you laid in this last year, and how many of those eggs ever hatched into chickens? The rest have all gone to market to bring in money for Jones and his men. And you, Clover, where are those four foals you bore, who should have been the support and pleasure of your old age? Each was sold at a year old—you will never see one of them again. In return for your four confinements and all your labour in the fields, what have you ever had except your bare rations and a stall?

"And even the miserable lives we lead are not allowed to reach their natural span. For myself I do not grumble, for I am one of the lucky ones. I am twelve years old and have had over four hundred children. Such is the natural life of a pig. But no animal escapes the cruel knife in the end. You young porkers who are sitting in front of me, every one of you will scream your lives out at the block within a year. To that horror we all must come—cows, pigs, hens, sheep, everyone. Even the horses and the dogs have no better fate. You, Boxer, the very day that those great muscles of yours lose their power, Jones will sell you to the knacker, who will cut your throat and boil you down for the foxhounds. As for the dogs, when they grow old and toothless, Jones ties a brick round their necks and drowns them in the nearest pond.

"Is it not crystal clear, then, comrades, that all the evils of this life of ours spring from the tyranny of human beings? Only get rid of Man, and the produce of our labour would be our own. Almost overnight we could become rich and free. What then must we do? Why, work night and day, body and soul, for the overthrow of the human race! That is my message to you, comrades: Rebellion! I do not know when that Rebellion will come, it might be in a week or in a hundred years, but I know, as surely as I see this straw beneath my feet, that sooner or later justice will be done. Fix your eyes on that, comrades, throughout the short remainder of your lives! And above all, pass on this message of mine to those who come after you, so that future generations shall carry on the struggle until it is victorious.

"And remember, comrades, your resolution must never falter. No argument must lead you astray. Never listen when they tell you that Man and the animals have a common interest, that the prosperity of the one is the prosperity of the others. It is all lies. Man serves the interests of no creature except himself. And among us animals let there be perfect unity, perfect comradeship in the struggle. All men are enemies. All animals are comrades."

At this moment there was a tremendous uproar. While Major was speaking four large rats had crept out of their holes and were sitting on their hindquarters, listening to him. The dogs had suddenly caught sight of them, and it was only by a swift dash for their holes that the rats saved their lives. Major raised his trotter for silence.

"Comrades," he said, "here is a point that must be settled. The wild creatures, such as rats and rabbits—are they our friends or our enemies? Let us put it to the vote. I propose this question to the meeting: Are rats comrades?"

The vote was taken at once, and it was agreed by an overwhelming majority that rats were comrades. There were only four dissentients, the three dogs and the cat, who was afterwards discovered to have voted on both sides. Major continued:

"I have little more to say. I merely repeat, remember always your duty of enmity towards Man and all his ways. Whatever goes upon two legs is an enemy. Whatever goes upon four legs, or has wings, is a friend. And remember also that in fighting against Man, we must not come to resemble him. Even when you have conquered him, do not adopt his vices. No animal must ever live in a house, or sleep in a bed, or wear clothes, or drink alcohol, or smoke tobacco, or touch money, or engage in trade. All the habits of Man are evil. And, above all, no animal must ever tyrannise over his own kind. Weak or strong, clever or simple, we are all brothers. No animal must ever kill any other animal. All animals are equal.

"And now, comrades, I will tell you about my dream of last night. I cannot describe that dream to you. It was a dream of the earth as it will be when Man has vanished. But it reminded me of something that I had long forgotten. Many years ago, when I was a little pig, my mother and the other sows used to sing an old song of which they knew only the tune and the first three words. I had known that tune in my infancy, but it had long since passed out of my mind. Last night, however, it came back to me in my dream. And what is more, the words of the song also came back—words, I am certain, which were sung by the animals of long ago and have been lost to memory for generations. I will sing you that song now, comrades. I am old and my voice is hoarse, but when I have taught you the tune, you can sing it better for yourselves. It is called 'Beasts of England'."

Old Major cleared his throat and began to sing. As he had said, his voice was hoarse, but he sang well enough, and it was a stirring tune, something between "Clementine" and "La Cucaracha". The words ran:

> Beasts of England, beasts of Ireland,
> Beasts of every land and clime,
> Hearken to my joyful tidings
> Of the golden future time.
>
> Soon or late the day is coming,
> Tyrant Man shall be o'erthrown,
> And the fruitful fields of England
> Shall be trod by beasts alone.
>
> Rings shall vanish from our noses,
> And the harness from our back,
> Bit and spur shall rust forever,
> Cruel whips no more shall crack.

Riches more than mind can picture,
Wheat and barley, oats and hay,
Clover, beans, and mangel-wurzels
Shall be ours upon that day.

Bright will shine the fields of England,
Purer shall its waters be,
Sweeter yet shall blow its breezes
On the day that sets us free.

For that day we all must labour,
Though we die before it break;
Cows and horses, geese and turkeys,
All must toil for freedom's sake.

Beasts of England, beasts of Ireland,
Beasts of every land and clime,
Hearken well and spread my tidings
Of the golden future time.

The singing of this song threw the animals into the wildest excitement. Almost before Major had reached the end, they had begun singing it for themselves. Even the stupidest of them had already picked up the tune and a few of the words, and as for the clever ones, such as the pigs and dogs, they had the entire song by heart within a few minutes. And then, after a few preliminary tries, the whole farm burst out into "Beasts of England" in tremendous unison. The cows lowed it, the dogs whined it, the sheep bleated it, the horses whinnied it, the ducks quacked it. They were so delighted with the song that they sang it right through five times in succession, and might have continued singing it all night if they had not been interrupted.

Unfortunately, the uproar awoke Mr. Jones, who sprang out of bed, making sure that there was a fox in the yard. He seized the gun which always stood in a corner of his bedroom, and let fly a charge of number 6 shot into the darkness. The pellets buried themselves in the wall of the barn and the meeting broke up hurriedly. Everyone fled to his own sleeping-place. The birds jumped on to their perches, the animals settled down in the straw, and the whole farm was asleep in a moment.

CHAPTER 2

Three nights later old Major died peacefully in his sleep. His body was buried at the foot of the orchard.

This was early in March. During the next three months there was much secret activity. Major's speech had given to the more intelligent animals on the farm a completely new outlook on life. They did not know when the Rebellion predicted by Major would take place, they had no reason for thinking that it would be within their own lifetime, but they saw clearly that it was their duty to prepare for it. The work of teaching and organising the others fell naturally upon the pigs, who were generally recognised as being the cleverest of the animals. Pre-eminent among the pigs were two young boars named Snowball and Napoleon, whom Mr. Jones was breeding up for sale. Napoleon was a large, rather fierce-looking Berkshire boar, the only Berkshire on the farm, not much of a talker, but with a reputation for getting his own way. Snowball was a more vivacious pig than Napoleon, quicker in speech and more inventive, but was not considered to have the same depth of character. All the other male pigs on the farm were porkers. The best known among them was a small fat pig named Squealer, with very round cheeks, twinkling eyes, nimble movements, and a shrill voice. He was a brilliant talker, and when he was arguing some difficult point he had a way of skipping from side to side and whisking his tail which was somehow very persuasive. The others said of Squealer that he could turn black into white.

These three had elaborated old Major's teachings into a complete system of thought, to which they gave the name of Animalism. Several nights a week, after Mr. Jones was asleep, they held secret meetings in the barn and expounded the principles of Animalism to the others. At the beginning they met with much stupidity and apathy. Some of the animals talked of the duty of loyalty to Mr. Jones, whom they referred to as "Master", or made elementary remarks such as "Mr. Jones feeds us. If he were gone, we should starve to death." Others asked such questions as "Why should we care what happens after we are dead?" or "If this Rebellion is to happen anyway, what difference does it make whether we work for it or not?", and the pigs had great difficulty in making them see that this was contrary to the spirit of Animalism. The stupidest questions of all were asked by Mollie, the white mare. The very first question she asked Snowball was: "Will there still be sugar after the Rebellion?"

"No," said Snowball firmly. "We have no means of making sugar on this farm. Besides, you do not need sugar. You will have all the oats and hay you want."

"And shall I still be allowed to wear ribbons in my mane?" asked Mollie.

"Comrade," said Snowball, "those ribbons that you are so devoted to are the badge of slavery. Can you not understand that liberty is worth more than ribbons?"

Mollie agreed, but she did not sound very convinced.

The pigs had an even harder struggle to counteract the lies put about by Moses, the tame raven. Moses, who was Mr. Jones's especial pet, was a spy and a tale-bearer, but he was also a clever talker. He claimed to know of the existence of a mysterious country called Sugarcandy Mountain, to which all animals went when they died. It was situated somewhere up in the sky, a little distance beyond the clouds, Moses said. In Sugarcandy Mountain it was Sunday seven days a week, clover was in season all the year round, and lump sugar and linseed cake grew on the hedges. The animals hated Moses because he told tales and did no work, but some of them believed in Sugarcandy Mountain, and the pigs had to argue very hard to persuade them that there was no such place.

Their most faithful disciples were the two cart-horses, Boxer and Clover. These two had great difficulty in thinking anything out for themselves, but having once accepted the pigs as their teachers, they absorbed everything that they were told, and passed it on to the other animals by simple arguments. They were unfailing in their attendance at the secret meetings in the barn, and led the singing of "Beasts of England", with which the meetings always ended.

Now, as it turned out, the Rebellion was achieved much earlier and more easily than anyone had expected. In past years Mr. Jones, although a hard master, had been a capable farmer, but of late he had fallen on evil days. He had become much disheartened after losing money in a lawsuit, and had taken to drinking more than was good for him. For whole days at a time he would lounge in his Windsor chair in the kitchen, reading the newspapers, drinking, and occasionally feeding Moses on crusts of bread soaked in beer. His men were idle and dishonest, the fields were full of weeds, the buildings wanted roofing, the hedges were neglected, and the animals were underfed.

June came and the hay was almost ready for cutting. On Midsummer's Eve, which was a Saturday, Mr. Jones went into Willingdon and got so drunk at the Red Lion that he did not come back till midday on Sunday. The men had milked the cows in the early morning and then had gone out rabbiting, without bothering to feed the animals. When Mr. Jones got back he immediately went to sleep on the drawing-room sofa with the *News of the World* over his face, so that when evening came, the animals were still unfed. At last they could stand it no longer. One of the cows broke in the door of the store-shed with her horn and all the animals began to help themselves from the bins. It was just then that Mr. Jones woke up. The next moment he and his four men were in the store-shed with whips in their hands, lashing out in all directions. This was more than the hungry animals could bear. With one accord, though nothing of the kind had been planned before-hand, they flung themselves upon their tormentors. Jones and his men suddenly found themselves being butted and kicked from all sides. The situation was quite out of their control. They had never seen animals behave like this before, and this sudden uprising of creatures whom they were used to thrashing and maltreating just as they chose, frightened them almost out of their wits. After only a moment or two they gave up trying to defend themselves and took to their heels. A minute later all five of them were in full flight down the cart-track that led to the main road, with the animals pursuing them in triumph.

Mrs. Jones looked out of the bedroom window, saw what was happening, hurriedly flung a few possessions into a carpet bag, and slipped out of the farm by another way. Moses sprang off his perch and flapped after her, croaking loudly. Meanwhile the animals had chased Jones and his men out on to the road and slammed the five-barred gate behind them. And so, almost before they knew what was happening, the Rebellion had been successfully carried through: Jones was expelled, and the Manor Farm was theirs.

For the first few minutes the animals could hardly believe in their good fortune. Their first act was to gallop in a body right round the boundaries of the farm, as though to make quite sure that no human being was hiding anywhere upon it; then they raced back to the farm buildings to wipe out the last traces of Jones's hated reign. The harness-room at the end of the stables was broken open; the bits, the nose-rings, the dog-chains, the cruel knives with which Mr. Jones had been used to castrate the pigs and lambs, were all flung down the well. The reins, the halters, the blinkers, the degrading nosebags, were thrown on to the rubbish fire which was burning in the yard. So were the whips. All the animals capered with joy when they saw the whips going up in flames. Snowball also threw on to the fire the ribbons with which the horses' manes and tails had usually been decorated on market days.

"Ribbons," he said, "should be considered as clothes, which are the mark of a human being. All animals should go naked."

When Boxer heard this he fetched the small straw hat which he wore in summer to keep the flies out of his ears, and flung it on to the fire with the rest.

In a very little while the animals had destroyed everything that reminded them of Mr. Jones. Napoleon then led them back to the store-shed and served out a double ration of corn to everybody, with two biscuits for each dog. Then they sang "Beasts of England" from end to end seven times running, and after that they settled down for the night and slept as they had never slept before.

But they woke at dawn as usual, and suddenly remembering the glorious thing that had happened, they all raced out into the pasture together. A little way down the pasture there was a knoll that commanded a view of most of the farm. The animals rushed to the top of it and gazed round them in the clear morning light. Yes, it was theirs—everything that they could see was theirs! In the ecstasy of that thought they gambolled round and round, they hurled themselves into the air in great leaps of excitement. They rolled in the dew, they cropped mouthfuls of the sweet summer grass, they kicked up clods of the black earth and snuffed its rich scent. Then they made a tour of inspection of the whole farm and surveyed with speechless admiration the ploughland, the hayfield, the orchard, the pool, the spinney. It was as though they had never seen these things before, and even now they could hardly believe that it was all their own.

Then they filed back to the farm buildings and halted in silence outside the door of the farmhouse. That was theirs too, but they were frightened to go inside. After a moment, however, Snowball and Napoleon butted the door open with their shoulders and the animals entered in single file, walking with the utmost care for fear of disturbing anything. They tiptoed from room to room, afraid to speak above a whisper and gazing with a kind of awe at the unbelievable luxury, at the beds with their feather mattresses, the looking-glasses, the horsehair sofa, the Brussels carpet, the lithograph of Queen Victoria over the drawing-room mantelpiece. They were just coming down the stairs when Mollie was discovered to be missing. Going back, the others found that she had remained behind in the best bedroom. She had taken a piece of blue ribbon from Mrs. Jones's dressing-table, and was holding it against her shoulder and admiring herself in the glass in a very foolish manner. The others reproached her sharply, and they went outside. Some hams hanging in the kitchen were taken out for burial, and the barrel of beer in the scullery was stove in with a kick from Boxer's hoof, otherwise nothing in the house was touched. A unanimous resolution was passed on the spot that the farmhouse should be preserved as a museum. All were agreed that no animal must ever live there.

The animals had their breakfast, and then Snowball and Napoleon called them together again.

"Comrades," said Snowball, "it is half-past six and we have a long day before us. Today we begin the hay harvest. But there is another matter that must be attended to first."

The pigs now revealed that during the past three months they had taught themselves to read and write from an old spelling book which had belonged to Mr. Jones's children and which had been thrown on the rubbish heap. Napoleon sent for pots of black and white paint and led the way down to the five-barred gate that gave on to the main road. Then Snowball (for it was Snowball who was best at writing) took a brush between the two knuckles of his trotter, painted out MANOR FARM from the top bar of the gate and in its place painted ANIMAL FARM. This was to be the name of the farm from now onwards. After this they went back to the farm buildings, where Snowball and Napoleon sent for a ladder which they caused to be set against the end wall of the big barn. They explained that by their studies of the past three months the pigs had succeeded in reducing the principles of Animalism to Seven Commandments. These Seven Commandments would now be inscribed on the wall; they would form an unalterable law by which all the animals on Animal Farm must live for ever after. With some difficulty (for it is not easy for a pig to balance himself on a ladder) Snowball climbed up and set to work, with Squealer a few rungs below him holding the paint-pot. The Commandments were written on the tarred wall in great white letters that could be read thirty yards away. They ran thus:

THE SEVEN COMMANDMENTS
1. *Whatever goes upon two legs is an enemy.*
2. *Whatever goes upon four legs, or has wings, is a friend.*
3. *No animal shall wear clothes.*
4. *No animal shall sleep in a bed.*
5. *No animal shall drink alcohol.*
6. *No animal shall kill any other animal.*
7. *All animals are equal.*

It was very neatly written, and except that "friend" was written "freind" and one of the S's was the wrong way round, the spelling was correct all the way through. Snowball read it aloud for the benefit of the others. All the animals nodded in complete agreement, and the cleverer ones at once began to learn the Commandments by heart.

"Now, comrades," cried Snowball, throwing down the paint-brush, "to the hayfield! Let us make it a point of honour to get in the harvest more quickly than Jones and his men could do."

But at this moment the three cows, who had seemed uneasy for some time past, set up a loud lowing. They had not been milked for twenty-four hours, and their udders were almost bursting. After a little thought, the pigs sent for buckets and milked the cows fairly successfully, their trotters being well adapted to this task. Soon there were five buckets of frothing creamy milk at which many of the animals looked with considerable interest.

"What is going to happen to all that milk?" said someone.

"Jones used sometimes to mix some of it in our mash," said one of the hens.

"Never mind the milk, comrades!" cried Napoleon, placing himself in front of the buckets. "That will be attended to. The harvest is more important. Comrade Snowball will lead the way. I shall follow in a few minutes. Forward, comrades! The hay is waiting."

So the animals trooped down to the hayfield to begin the harvest, and when they came back in the evening it was noticed that the milk had disappeared.

CHAPTER 3

How they toiled and sweated to get the hay in! But their efforts were rewarded, for the harvest was an even bigger success than they had hoped.

Sometimes the work was hard; the implements had been designed for human beings and not for animals, and it was a great drawback that no animal was able to use any tool that involved standing on his hind legs. But the pigs were so clever that they could think of a way round every difficulty. As for the horses, they knew every inch of the field, and in fact understood the business of mowing and raking far better than Jones and his men had ever done. The pigs did not actually work, but directed and supervised the others. With their superior knowledge it was natural that they should assume the leadership. Boxer and Clover would harness themselves to the cutter or the horse-rake (no bits or reins were needed in these days, of course) and tramp steadily round and round the field with a pig walking behind and calling out "Gee up, comrade!" or "Whoa back, comrade!" as the case might be. And every animal down to the humblest worked at turning the hay and gathering it. Even the ducks and hens toiled to and fro all day in the sun, carrying tiny wisps of hay in their beaks. In the end they finished the harvest in two days' less time than it had usually taken Jones and his men. Moreover, it was the biggest harvest that the farm had ever seen. There was no wastage whatever; the hens and ducks with their sharp eyes had gathered up the very last stalk. And not an animal on the farm had stolen so much as a mouthful.

All through that summer the work of the farm went like clockwork. The animals were happy as they had never conceived it possible to be. Every mouthful of food was an acute positive pleasure, now that it was truly their own food, produced by themselves and for themselves, not doled out to them by a grudging master. With the worthless parasitical human beings gone, there was more for everyone to eat. There was more leisure too, inexperienced though the animals were. They met with many difficulties—for instance, later in the year, when they harvested the corn, they had to tread it out in the ancient style and blow away the chaff with their breath, since the farm possessed no threshing machine—but the pigs with their cleverness and Boxer with his tremendous muscles always pulled them through. Boxer was the admiration of everybody. He had been a hard worker even in Jones's time, but now he seemed more like three horses than one; there were days when the entire work of the farm seemed to rest on his mighty shoulders. From morning to night he was pushing and pulling, always at the spot where the work was hardest. He had made an arrangement with one of the cockerels to call him in the mornings half an hour earlier than anyone else, and would put in some volunteer labour at whatever seemed to be most needed, before the regular day's work began. His answer to every problem, every setback, was "I will work harder!"—which he had adopted as his personal motto.

But everyone worked according to his capacity. The hens and ducks, for instance, saved five bushels of corn at the harvest by gathering up the stray grains. Nobody stole, nobody grumbled over his rations, the quarrelling and biting and jealousy which had been normal features of life in the old days had almost disappeared. Nobody shirked—or almost nobody. Mollie, it was true, was not good at getting up in the mornings, and had a way of leaving work early on the ground that there was a stone in her hoof. And the behaviour of the cat was somewhat peculiar. It was soon noticed that when there was work to be done the cat could never be found. She would vanish for hours on end, and then reappear at meal-times, or in the evening after work was over, as though nothing had happened. But she always made such excellent excuses, and purred so affectionately, that it was impossible not to believe in her good intentions. Old Benjamin, the donkey, seemed quite unchanged since the Rebellion. He did his work in the same slow obstinate way as he had done it in Jones's time, never shirking and never volunteering for extra work either. About the Rebellion and its results he would express no opinion. When asked whether he was not happier now that Jones was gone, he would say only "Donkeys live a long time. None of you has ever seen a dead donkey," and the others had to be content with this cryptic answer.

On Sundays there was no work. Breakfast was an hour later than usual, and after breakfast there was a ceremony which was observed every week without fail. First came the hoisting of the flag. Snowball had found in the harness-room an old green tablecloth of Mrs. Jones's and had painted on it a hoof and a horn in white. This was run up the flagstaff in the farmhouse garden every Sunday morning. The flag was green, Snowball explained, to represent the green fields of England, while the hoof and horn signified the future Republic of the Animals which would arise when the human race had been finally overthrown. After the hoisting of the flag all the animals trooped into the big barn for a general assembly which was known as the Meeting. Here the work of the coming week was planned out and resolutions were put forward and debated. It was always the pigs who put forward the resolutions. The other animals understood how to vote, but could never think of any resolutions of their own. Snowball and Napoleon were by far the most active in the debates. But it was noticed that these two were never in agreement: whatever suggestion either of them made, the other could be counted on to oppose it. Even when it was resolved—a thing no one could object to in itself—to set aside the small paddock behind the orchard as a home of rest for animals who were past work, there was a stormy debate over the correct retiring age for each class of animal. The Meeting always ended with the singing of "Beasts of England", and the afternoon was given up to recreation.

The pigs had set aside the harness-room as a headquarters for themselves. Here, in the evenings, they studied blacksmithing, carpentering, and other necessary arts from books which they had brought out of the farmhouse. Snowball also busied himself with organising the other animals into what he called Animal Committees. He was indefatigable at this. He formed the Egg Production Committee for the hens, the Clean Tails League for the cows, the Wild Comrades' Re-education Committee (the object of this was to tame the rats and rabbits), the Whiter Wool Movement for the sheep, and various others, besides instituting classes in reading and writing. On the whole, these projects were a failure. The attempt to tame the wild creatures, for instance, broke down almost immediately. They continued to behave very much as before, and when treated with generosity, simply took advantage of it. The cat joined the Re-education Committee and was very active in it for some days. She was seen one day sitting on a roof and talking to some sparrows who were just out of her reach. She was telling them that all animals were now comrades and that any sparrow who chose could come and perch on her paw; but the sparrows kept their distance.

The reading and writing classes, however, were a great success. By the autumn almost every animal on the farm was literate in some degree.

As for the pigs, they could already read and write perfectly. The dogs learned to read fairly well, but were not interested in reading anything except the Seven Commandments. Muriel, the goat, could read somewhat better than the dogs, and sometimes used to read to the others in the evenings from scraps of newspaper which she found on the rubbish heap. Benjamin could read as well as any pig, but never exercised his faculty. So far as he knew, he said, there was nothing worth reading. Clover learnt the whole alphabet, but could not put words together. Boxer could not get beyond the letter D. He would trace out A, B, C, D, in the dust with his great hoof, and then would stand staring at the letters with his ears back, sometimes shaking his forelock, trying with all his might to remember what came next and never succeeding. On several occasions, indeed, he did learn E, F, G, H, but by the time he knew them, it was always discovered that he had forgotten A, B, C, and D. Finally he decided to be content with the first four letters, and used to write them out once or twice every day to refresh his memory. Mollie refused to learn any but the six letters which spelt her own name. She would form these very neatly out of pieces of twig, and would then decorate them with a flower or two and walk round them admiring them.

None of the other animals on the farm could get further than the letter A. It was also found that the stupider animals, such as the sheep, hens, and ducks, were unable to learn the Seven Commandments by heart. After much thought Snowball declared that the Seven Commandments could in effect be reduced to a single maxim, namely: "Four legs good, two legs bad." This, he said, contained the essential principle of Animalism. Whoever had thoroughly grasped it would be safe from human influences. The birds at first objected, since it seemed to them that they also had two legs, but Snowball proved to them that this was not so.

"A bird's wing, comrades," he said, "is an organ of propulsion and not of manipulation. It should therefore be regarded as a leg. The distinguishing mark of man is the *hand*, the instrument with which he does all his mischief."

The birds did not understand Snowball's long words, but they accepted his explanation, and all the humbler animals set to work to learn the new maxim by heart. FOUR LEGS GOOD, TWO LEGS BAD, was inscribed on the end wall of the barn, above the Seven Commandments and in bigger letters. When they had once got it by heart, the sheep developed a great liking for this maxim, and often as they lay in the field they would all start bleating "Four legs good, two legs bad! Four legs good, two legs bad!" and keep it up for hours on end, never growing tired of it.

Napoleon took no interest in Snowball's committees. He said that the education of the young was more important than anything that could be done for those who were already grown up. It happened that Jessie and Bluebell had both whelped soon after the hay harvest, giving birth between them to nine sturdy puppies. As soon as they were weaned, Napoleon took them away from their mothers, saying that he would make himself responsible for their education. He took them up into a loft which could only be reached by a ladder from the harness-room, and there kept them in such seclusion that the rest of the farm soon forgot their existence.

The mystery of where the milk went to was soon cleared up. It was mixed every day into the pigs' mash. The early apples were now ripening, and the grass of the orchard was littered with windfalls. The animals had assumed as a matter of course that these would be shared out equally; one day, however, the order went forth that all the windfalls were to be collected and brought to the harness-room for the use of the pigs. At this some of the other animals murmured, but it was no use. All the pigs were in full agreement on this point, even Snowball and Napoleon. Squealer was sent to make the necessary explanations to the others.

"Comrades!" he cried. "You do not imagine, I hope, that

we pigs are doing this in a spirit of selfishness and privilege? Many of us actually dislike milk and apples. I dislike them myself. Our sole object in taking these things is to preserve our health. Milk and apples (this has been proved by Science, comrades) contain substances absolutely necessary to the well-being of a pig. We pigs are brainworkers. The whole management and organisation of this farm depend on us. Day and night we are watching over your welfare. It is for *your* sake that we drink that milk and eat those apples. Do you know what would happen if we pigs failed in our duty? Jones would come back! Yes, Jones would come back! Surely, comrades," cried Squealer almost pleadingly, skipping from side to side and whisking his tail, "surely there is no one among you who wants to see Jones come back?"

Now if there was one thing that the animals were completely certain of, it was that they did not want Jones back. When it was put to them in this light, they had no more to say. The importance of keeping the pigs in good health was all too obvious. So it was agreed without further argument that the milk and the windfall apples (and also the main crop of apples when they ripened) should be reserved for the pigs alone.

CHAPTER 4

By the late summer the news of what had happened on Animal Farm had spread across half the county. Every day Snowball and Napoleon sent out flights of pigeons whose instructions were to mingle with the animals on neighbouring farms, tell them the story of the Rebellion, and teach them the tune of "Beasts of England".

Most of this time Mr. Jones had spent sitting in the taproom of the Red Lion at Willingdon, complaining to anyone who would listen of the monstrous injustice he had suffered in being turned out of his property by a pack of good-for-nothing animals. The other farmers sympathised in principle, but they did not at first give him much help. At heart, each of them was secretly wondering whether he could not somehow turn Jones's misfortune to his own advantage. It was lucky that the owners of the two farms which adjoined Animal Farm were on permanently bad terms. One of them, which was named Foxwood, was a large, neglected, old-fashioned farm, much overgrown by woodland, with all its pastures worn out and its hedges in a disgraceful condition. Its owner, Mr. Pilkington, was an easy-going gentleman farmer who spent most of his time in fishing or hunting according to the season. The other farm, which was called Pinchfield, was smaller and better kept. Its owner was a Mr. Frederick, a tough, shrewd man, perpetually involved in lawsuits and with a name for driving hard bargains. These two disliked each other so much that it was difficult for them to come to any agreement, even in defence of their own interests.

Nevertheless, they were both thoroughly frightened by the rebellion on Animal Farm, and very anxious to prevent their own animals from learning too much about it. At first they pretended to laugh to scorn the idea of animals managing a farm for themselves. The whole thing would be over in a fortnight, they said. They put it about that the animals on the Manor Farm (they insisted on calling it the Manor Farm; they would not tolerate the name "Animal Farm") were perpetually fighting among themselves and were also rapidly starving to death. When time passed and the animals had evidently not starved to death, Frederick and Pilkington changed their tune and began to talk of the terrible wickedness that now flourished on Animal Farm. It was given out that the animals there practised cannibalism, tortured one another with red-hot horseshoes, and had their females in common. This was what came of rebelling against the laws of Nature, Frederick and Pilkington said.

However, these stories were never fully believed. Rumours of a wonderful farm, where the human beings had been turned out and the animals managed their own affairs, continued to circulate in vague and distorted forms, and throughout that year a wave of rebelliousness ran through the countryside. Bulls which had always been tractable suddenly turned savage, sheep broke down hedges and devoured the clover, cows kicked the pail over, hunters refused their fences and shot their riders on to the other side. Above all, the tune and even the words of "Beasts of England" were known everywhere. It had spread with astonishing speed. The human beings could not contain their rage when they heard this song, though they pretended to think it merely ridiculous. They could not understand, they said, how even animals could bring themselves to sing such contemptible rubbish. Any animal caught singing it was given a flogging on the spot. And yet the song was irrepressible. The blackbirds whistled it in the hedges, the pigeons cooed it in the elms, it got into the din of the smithies and the tune of the church bells. And when the human beings listened to it, they secretly trembled, hearing in it a prophecy of their future doom.

Early in October, when the corn was cut and stacked and some of it was already threshed, a flight of pigeons came whirling through the air and alighted in the yard of Animal Farm in the wildest excitement. Jones and all his men, with half a dozen others from Foxwood and Pinchfield, had entered the five-barred gate and were coming up the cart-track that led to the farm. They were all carrying sticks, except Jones, who was marching ahead with a gun in his hands. Obviously they were going to attempt the recapture of the farm.

This had long been expected, and all preparations had been made. Snowball, who had studied an old book of Julius Caesar's campaigns which he had found in the farmhouse, was in charge of the defensive operations. He gave his orders quickly, and in a couple of minutes every animal was at his post.

As the human beings approached the farm buildings, Snowball launched his first attack. All the pigeons, to the number of thirty-five, flew to and fro over the men's heads and muted upon them from mid-air; and while the men were dealing with this, the geese, who had been hiding behind the hedge, rushed out and pecked viciously at the calves of their legs. However, this was only a light skirmishing manoeuvre, intended to create a little disorder, and the men easily drove the geese off with their sticks. Snowball now launched his second line of attack. Muriel, Benjamin, and all the sheep, with Snowball at the head of them, rushed forward and prodded and butted the men from every side, while Benjamin turned around and lashed at them with his small hoofs. But once again the men, with their sticks and their hobnailed boots, were too strong for them; and suddenly, at a squeal from Snowball, which was the signal for retreat, all the animals turned and fled through the gateway into the yard.

The men gave a shout of triumph. They saw, as they imagined, their enemies in flight, and they rushed after them in disorder. This was just what Snowball had intended. As soon as they were well inside the yard, the three horses, the three cows, and the rest of the pigs, who had been lying in ambush in the cowshed, suddenly emerged in their rear, cutting them off. Snowball now gave the signal for the charge. He himself dashed straight for Jones. Jones saw him coming, raised his gun and fired. The pellets scored bloody streaks along Snowball's back, and a sheep dropped dead. Without halting for an instant, Snowball flung his fifteen stone against Jones's legs. Jones was hurled into a pile of dung and his gun flew out of his hands. But the most terrifying spectacle of all was Boxer, rearing up on his hind legs and striking out with his great iron-shod hoofs like a stallion. His very first blow took a stable-lad from Foxwood on the skull and stretched him lifeless in the mud. At the sight, several men dropped their sticks and tried to run. Panic overtook them, and the next moment all the animals together were chasing them round and round the yard. They were gored, kicked, bitten, trampled on. There was not an animal on the farm that did not take vengeance on them after his own fashion. Even the cat suddenly leapt off a roof onto a cowman's shoulders and sank her claws in his neck, at which he yelled horribly. At a moment when the opening was clear, the men were glad enough to rush out of the yard and make a bolt for the main road. And so within five minutes of their invasion they were in ignominious retreat by the same way as they had come, with a flock of geese hissing after them and pecking at their calves all the way.

All the men were gone except one. Back in the yard Boxer was pawing with his hoof at the stable-lad who lay face down in the mud, trying to turn him over. The boy did not stir.

"He is dead," said Boxer sorrowfully. "I had no intention of doing that. I forgot that I was wearing iron shoes. Who will believe that I did not do this on purpose?"

"No sentimentality, comrade!" cried Snowball from whose wounds the blood was still dripping. "War is war. The only good human being is a dead one."

"I have no wish to take life, not even human life," repeated Boxer, and his eyes were full of tears.

"Where is Mollie?" exclaimed somebody.

Mollie in fact was missing. For a moment there was great alarm; it was feared that the men might have harmed her in some way, or even carried her off with them. In the end, however, she was found hiding in her stall with her head buried among the hay in the manger. She had taken to flight as soon as the gun went off. And when the others came back from looking for her, it was to find that the stable-lad, who in fact was only stunned, had already recovered and made off.

The animals had now reassembled in the wildest excitement, each recounting his own exploits in the battle at the top of his voice. An impromptu celebration of the victory was held immediately. The flag was run up and "Beasts of England" was sung a number of times, then the sheep who had been killed was given a solemn funeral, a hawthorn bush being planted on her grave. At the graveside Snowball made a little speech, emphasising the need for all animals to be ready to die for Animal Farm if need be.

The animals decided unanimously to create a military decoration, "Animal Hero, First Class", which was conferred there and then on Snowball and Boxer. It consisted of a brass medal (they were really some old horse brasses which had been found in the harness-room), to be worn on Sundays and holidays. There was also "Animal Hero, Second Class", which was conferred posthumously on the dead sheep.

There was much discussion as to what the battle should be called. In the end, it was named the Battle of the Cowshed, since that was where the ambush had been sprung. Mr. Jones's gun had been found lying in the mud, and it was known that there was a supply of cartridges in the farmhouse. It was decided to set the gun up at the foot of the flagstaff, like a piece of artillery, and to fire it twice a year—once on October the twelfth, the anniversary of the Battle of the Cowshed, and once on Midsummer Day, the anniversary of the Rebellion.

CHAPTER 5

As winter drew on, Mollie became more and more trouble-some. She was late for work every morning and excused herself by saying that she had overslept, and she complained of myste-rious pains, although her appetite was excellent. On every kind of pretext she would run away from work and go to the drinking pool, where she would stand foolishly gazing at her own reflection in the water. But there were also rumours of something more serious. One day, as Mollie strolled blithely into the yard, flirting her long tail and chewing at a stalk of hay, Clover took her aside.

"Mollie," she said, "I have something very serious to say to you. This morning I saw you looking over the hedge that divides Animal Farm from Foxwood. One of Mr. Pilkington's men was standing on the other side of the hedge. And—I was a long way away, but I am almost certain I saw this—he was talking to you and you were allowing him to stroke your nose. What does that mean, Mollie?"

"He didn't! I wasn't! It isn't true!" cried Mollie, begin-ning to prance about and paw the ground.

"Mollie! Look me in the face. Do you give me your word of honour that that man was not stroking your nose?"

"It isn't true!" repeated Mollie, but she could not look

Clover in the face, and the next moment she took to her heels and galloped away into the field.

A thought struck Clover. Without saying anything to the others, she went to Mollie's stall and turned over the straw with her hoof. Hidden under the straw was a little pile of lump sugar and several bunches of ribbon of different colours.

Three days later Mollie disappeared. For some weeks nothing was known of her whereabouts, then the pigeons reported that they had seen her on the other side of Willingdon. She was between the shafts of a smart dogcart painted red and black, which was standing outside a public-house. A fat red-faced man in check breeches and gaiters, who looked like a publican, was stroking her nose and feeding her with sugar. Her coat was newly clipped and she wore a scarlet ribbon round her forelock. She appeared to be enjoying herself, so the pigeons said. None of the animals ever mentioned Mollie again.

In January there came bitterly hard weather. The earth was like iron, and nothing could be done in the fields. Many meetings were held in the big barn, and the pigs occupied themselves with planning out the work of the coming season. It had come to be accepted that the pigs, who were manifestly cleverer than the other animals, should decide all questions of farm policy, though their decisions had to be ratified by a majority vote. This arrangement would have worked well enough if it had not been for the disputes between Snowball and Napoleon. These two disagreed at every point where disagreement was possible. If one of them suggested sowing a bigger acreage with barley, the other was certain to demand a bigger acreage of oats, and if one of them said that such and such a field was just right for cabbages, the other would declare that it was useless for anything except roots. Each had his own following, and there were some violent debates. At the Meetings Snowball often won over the majority by his brilliant speeches, but Napoleon was better at canvassing support for himself in between times. He was especially successful with the sheep. Of late the sheep had taken to bleating "Four legs good, two legs bad" both in and out of season, and they often interrupted the Meeting with this. It was noticed that they were especially liable to break into "Four legs good, two legs bad" at crucial moments in Snowball's speeches. Snowball had made a close study of some back numbers of the *Farmer and Stockbreeder* which he had found in the farmhouse, and was full of plans for innovations and improvements. He talked learnedly about field drains, silage, and basic slag, and had worked out a complicated scheme for all the animals to drop their dung directly in the fields, at a different spot every day, to save the labour of cartage. Napoleon produced no schemes of his own, but said quietly that Snowball's would come to nothing, and seemed to be biding his time. But of all their controversies, none was so bitter as the one that took place over the windmill.

In the long pasture, not far from the farm buildings, there was a small knoll which was the highest point on the farm. After surveying the ground, Snowball declared that this was just the place for a windmill, which could be made to operate a dynamo and supply the farm with electrical power. This would light the stalls and warm them in winter, and would also run a circular saw, a chaff-cutter, a mangel-slicer, and an electric milking machine. The animals had never heard of anything of this kind before (for the farm was an old-fashioned one and had only the most primitive machinery), and they listened in astonishment while Snowball conjured up pictures of fantastic machines which would do their work for them while they grazed at their ease in the fields or improved their minds with reading and conversation.

Within a few weeks Snowball's plans for the windmill were fully worked out. The mechanical details came mostly from three books which had belonged to Mr. Jones—*One Thousand Useful Things to Do About the House, Every Man*

His Own Bricklayer, and *Electricity for Beginners*. Snowball used as his study a shed which had once been used for incubators and had a smooth wooden floor, suitable for drawing on. He was closeted there for hours at a time. With his books held open by a stone, and with a piece of chalk gripped between the knuckles of his trotter, he would move rapidly to and fro, drawing in line after line and uttering little whimpers of excitement. Gradually the plans grew into a complicated mass of cranks and cog-wheels, covering more than half the floor, which the other animals found completely unintelligible but very impressive. All of them came to look at Snowball's drawings at least once a day. Even the hens and ducks came, and were at pains not to tread on the chalk marks. Only Napoleon held aloof. He had declared himself against the windmill from the start. One day, however, he arrived unexpectedly to examine the plans. He walked heavily round the shed, looked closely at every detail of the plans and snuffed at them once or twice, then stood for a little while contemplating them out of the corner of his eye; then suddenly he lifted his leg, urinated over the plans, and walked out without uttering a word.

The whole farm was deeply divided on the subject of the windmill. Snowball did not deny that to build it would be a difficult business. Stone would have to be quarried and built up into walls, then the sails would have to be made and after that there would be need for dynamos and cables. (How these were to be procured, Snowball did not say.) But he maintained that it could all be done in a year. And thereafter, he declared, so much labour would be saved that the animals would only need to work three days a week. Napoleon, on the other hand, argued that the great need of the moment was to increase food production, and that if they wasted time on the windmill they would all starve to death. The animals formed themselves into two factions under the slogan, "Vote for Snowball and the three-day week" and "Vote for Napoleon and the full manger". Benjamin was the only animal who did not side with either faction. He refused to believe either that food would become more plentiful or that the windmill would save work. Windmill or no windmill, he said, life would go on as it had always gone on—that is, badly.

Apart from the disputes over the windmill, there was the question of the defence of the farm. It was fully realised that though the human beings had been defeated in the Battle of the Cowshed they might make another and more determined attempt to recapture the farm and reinstate Mr. Jones. They had all the more reason for doing so because the news of their defeat had spread across the countryside and made the animals on the neighbouring farms more restive than ever. As usual, Snowball and Napoleon were in disagreement. According to Napoleon, what the animals must do was to procure firearms and train themselves in the use of them. According to Snowball, they must send out more and more pigeons and stir up rebellion among the animals on the other farms. The one argued that if they could not defend themselves they were bound to be conquered, the other argued that if rebellion happened everywhere they would have no need to defend themselves. The animals listened first to Napoleon, then to Snowball, and could not make up their minds which was right; indeed, they always found themselves in agreement with the one who was speaking at the moment.

At last the day came when Snowball's plans were completed. At the Meeting on the following Sunday the question of whether or not to begin work on the windmill was to be put to the vote. When the animals had assembled in the big barn, Snowball stood up and, though occasionally interrupted by bleating from the sheep, set forth his reasons for advocating the building of the windmill. Then Napoleon stood up to reply. He said very quietly that the windmill was nonsense and that he advised nobody to vote for it, and promptly sat down again; he had spoken for barely thirty seconds, and seemed almost indifferent as to the effect he produced. At this Snowball sprang to his feet, and shouting down the sheep, who had begun bleating again, broke into a passionate appeal in favour of the windmill. Until now the animals had been about equally divided in their sympathies, but in a moment Snowball's eloquence had carried them away. In glowing sentences he painted a picture of Animal Farm as it might be when sordid labour was lifted from the animals' backs. His imagination had now run far beyond chaff-cutters and turnip-slicers. Electricity, he said, could operate threshing machines, ploughs, harrows, rollers, and reapers and binders, besides supplying every stall with its own electric light, hot and cold water, and an electric heater. By the time he had finished speaking, there was no doubt as to which way the vote would go. But just at this moment Napoleon stood up and, casting a peculiar sidelong look at Snowball, uttered a high-pitched whimper of a kind no one had ever heard him utter before.

At this there was a terrible baying sound outside, and nine enormous dogs wearing brass-studded collars came bounding into the barn. They dashed straight for Snowball, who only sprang from his place just in time to escape their snapping jaws. In a moment he was out of the door and they were after him. Too amazed and frightened to speak, all the animals crowded through the door to watch the chase. Snowball was racing across the long pasture that led to the road. He was running as only a pig can run, but the dogs were close on his heels. Suddenly he slipped and it seemed certain that they had him. Then he was up again, running faster than ever, then the dogs were gaining on him again. One of them all but closed his jaws on Snowball's tail, but Snowball whisked it free just in time. Then he put on an extra spurt and, with a few inches to spare, slipped through a hole in the hedge and was seen no more.

Silent and terrified, the animals crept back into the barn.

In a moment the dogs came bounding back. At first no one had been able to imagine where these creatures came from, but the problem was soon solved: they were the puppies whom Napoleon had taken away from their mothers and reared privately. Though not yet full-grown, they were huge dogs, and as fierce-looking as wolves. They kept close to Napoleon. It was noticed that they wagged their tails to him in the same way as the other dogs had been used to do to Mr. Jones.

Napoleon, with the dogs following him, now mounted on to the raised portion of the floor where Major had previously stood to deliver his speech. He announced that from now on the Sunday-morning Meetings would come to an end. They were unnecessary, he said, and wasted time. In future all questions relating to the working of the farm would be settled by a special committee of pigs, presided over by himself. These would meet in private and afterwards communicate their decisions to the others. The animals would still assemble on Sunday mornings to salute the flag, sing "Beasts of England", and receive their orders for the week; but there would be no more debates.

In spite of the shock that Snowball's expulsion had given them, the animals were dismayed by this announcement. Several of them would have protested if they could have found the right arguments. Even Boxer was vaguely troubled. He set his ears back, shook his forelock several times, and tried hard to marshal his thoughts; but in the end he could not think of anything to say. Some of the pigs themselves, however, were more articulate. Four young porkers in the front row uttered shrill squeals of disapproval, and all four of them sprang to their feet and began speaking at once. But suddenly the dogs sitting round Napoleon let out deep, menacing growls, and the pigs fell silent and sat down again. Then the sheep broke out into a tremendous bleating of "Four legs good, two legs bad!" which went on for nearly a quarter of an hour and put an end to any chance of discussion.

Afterwards Squealer was sent round the farm to explain the new arrangement to the others.

"Comrades," he said, "I trust that every animal here appreciates the sacrifice that Comrade Napoleon has made in taking this extra labour upon himself. Do not imagine, comrades, that leadership is a pleasure! On the contrary, it is a deep and heavy responsibility. No one believes more firmly than Comrade Napoleon that all animals are equal. He would be only too happy to let you make your decisions for yourselves. But sometimes you might make the wrong decisions, comrades, and then where should we be? Suppose you had decided to follow Snowball, with his moonshine of windmills—Snowball, who, as we now know, was no better than a criminal?"

"He fought bravely at the Battle of the Cowshed," said somebody.

"Bravery is not enough," said Squealer. "Loyalty and obedience are more important. And as to the Battle of the Cowshed, I believe the time will come when we shall find that Snowball's part in it was much exaggerated. Discipline, comrades, iron discipline! That is the watchword for today. One false step, and our enemies would be upon us. Surely, comrades, you do not want Jones back?"

Once again this argument was unanswerable. Certainly the animals did not want Jones back; if the holding of debates on Sunday mornings was liable to bring him back, then the debates must stop. Boxer, who had now had time to think things over, voiced the general feeling by saying: "If Comrade Napoleon says it, it must be right." And from then on he adopted the maxim, "Napoleon is always right", in addition to his private motto of "I will work harder".

By this time the weather had broken and the spring ploughing had begun. The shed where Snowball had drawn his plans of the windmill had been shut up and it was assumed that the plans had been rubbed off the floor. Every Sunday morning at ten o'clock the animals assembled in the big barn to receive their orders for the week. The skull of old Major, now clean of flesh, had been disinterred from the orchard and set up on a stump at the foot of the flagstaff, beside the gun. After the hoisting of the flag, the animals were required to file past the skull in a reverent manner before entering the barn. Nowadays they did not sit all together as they had done in the past. Napoleon, with Squealer and another pig named Minimus, who had a remarkable gift for composing songs and poems, sat on the front of the raised platform, with the nine young dogs forming a semicircle round them, and the other pigs sitting behind. The rest of the animals sat facing them in the main body of the barn. Napoleon read out the orders for the week in a gruff soldierly style, and after a single singing of "Beasts of England", all the animals dispersed.

On the third Sunday after Snowball's expulsion, the animals were somewhat surprised to hear Napoleon announce that the windmill was to be built after all. He did not give any reason for having changed his mind, but merely warned the animals that this extra task would mean very hard work, it might even be necessary to reduce their rations. The plans, however, had all been prepared, down to the last detail. A special committee of pigs had been at work upon them for the past three weeks. The building of the windmill, with various other improvements, was expected to take two years.

That evening Squealer explained privately to the other animals that Napoleon had never in reality been opposed to the windmill. On the contrary, it was he who had advocated it in the beginning, and the plan which Snowball had drawn on the floor of the incubator shed had actually been stolen from among Napoleon's papers. The windmill was, in fact, Napoleon's own creation. Why, then, asked somebody, had he spoken so strongly against it? Here Squealer looked very sly. That, he said, was Comrade Napoleon's cunning. He had *seemed* to oppose the windmill, simply as a manoeuvre to get rid of Snowball, who was a dangerous character and a bad influence. Now that Snowball was out of the way, the plan could go forward without his interference. This, said Squealer, was something called tactics. He repeated a number of times, "Tactics, comrades, tactics!" skipping round and whisking his tail with a merry laugh. The animals were not certain what the word meant, but Squealer spoke so persuasively, and the three dogs who happened to be with him growled so threateningly, that they accepted his explanation without further questions.

CHAPTER 6

All that year the animals worked like slaves. But they were happy in their work; they grudged no effort or sacrifice, well aware that everything that they did was for the benefit of themselves and those of their kind who would come after them, and not for a pack of idle, thieving human beings.

Throughout the spring and summer they worked a sixty-hour week, and in August Napoleon announced that there would be work on Sunday afternoons as well. This work was strictly voluntary, but any animal who absented himself from it would have his rations reduced by half. Even so, it was found necessary to leave certain tasks undone. The harvest was a little less successful than in the previous year, and two fields which should have been sown with roots in the early summer were not sown because the ploughing had not been completed early enough. It was possible to foresee that the coming winter would be a hard one.

The windmill presented unexpected difficulties. There was a good quarry of limestone on the farm, and plenty of sand and cement had been found in one of the outhouses, so that all the materials for building were at hand. But the problem the animals could not at first solve was how to break up the stone into pieces of suitable size. There seemed no way of doing this except with picks and crowbars, which no animal could use, because no animal could stand on his hind legs. Only after weeks of vain effort did the right idea occur to somebody—namely, to utilise the force of gravity. Huge boulders, far too big to be used as they were, were lying all over the bed of the quarry. The animals lashed ropes round these, and then all together, cows, horses, sheep, any animal that could lay hold of the rope—even the pigs sometimes joined in at critical moments—they dragged them with desperate slowness up the slope to the top of the quarry, where they were toppled over the edge, to shatter to pieces below. Transporting the stone when it was once broken was comparatively simple. The horses carried it off in cart-loads, the sheep dragged single blocks, even Muriel and Benjamin yoked themselves into an old governess-cart and did their share. By late summer a sufficient store of stone had accumulated, and then the building began, under the superintendence of the pigs.

But it was a slow, laborious process. Frequently it took a whole day of exhausting effort to drag a single boulder to the top of the quarry, and sometimes when it was pushed over the edge it failed to break. Nothing could have been achieved without Boxer, whose strength seemed equal to that of all the rest of the animals put together. When the boulder began to slip and the animals cried out in despair at finding themselves dragged down the hill, it was always Boxer who strained himself against the rope and brought the boulder to a stop. To see him toiling up the slope inch by inch, his breath coming fast, the tips of his hoofs clawing at the ground, and his great sides matted with sweat, filled everyone with admiration. Clover warned him sometimes to be careful not to overstrain himself, but Boxer would never listen to her. His two slogans, "I will work harder" and "Napoleon is always right", seemed to him a sufficient answer to all problems. He had made arrangements with the cockerel to call him three-quarters of an hour earlier in the mornings instead of half an hour. And in his spare moments, of which there were not many nowadays, he would go alone to the quarry, collect a load of broken stone, and drag it down to the site of the windmill unassisted.

The animals were not badly off throughout that summer, in spite of the hardness of their work. If they had no more food than they had had in Jones's day, at least they did not have less. The advantage of only having to feed themselves, and not having to support five extravagant human beings as well, was so great that it would have taken a lot of failures to outweigh it. And in many ways the animal method of doing things was more efficient and saved labour. Such jobs as weeding, for instance, could be done with a thoroughness impossible to human beings. And again, since no animal now stole, it was unnecessary to fence off pasture from arable land, which saved a lot of labour on the upkeep of hedges and gates. Nevertheless, as the summer wore on, various unforeseen shortages began to make themselves felt. There was need of paraffin oil, nails, string, dog biscuits, and iron for the horses' shoes, none of which could be produced on the farm. Later there would also be need for seeds and artificial manures, besides various tools and, finally, the machinery for the windmill. How these were to be procured, no one was able to imagine.

One Sunday morning, when the animals assembled to receive their orders, Napoleon announced that he had decided upon a new policy. From now onwards Animal Farm would engage in trade with the neighbouring farms: not, of course, for any commercial purpose, but simply in order to obtain certain materials which were urgently necessary. The needs of the windmill must override everything else, he said. He was therefore making arrangements to sell a stack of hay and part of the current year's wheat crop, and later on, if more money were needed, it would have to be made up by the sale of eggs, for which there was always a market in Willingdon.

The hens, said Napoleon, should welcome this sacrifice as their own special contribution towards the building of the windmill.

Once again the animals were conscious of a vague uneasiness. Never to have any dealings with human beings, never to engage in trade, never to make use of money—had not these been among the earliest resolutions passed at that first triumphant Meeting after Jones was expelled? All the animals remembered passing such resolutions: or at least they thought that they remembered it. The four young pigs who had protested when Napoleon abolished the Meetings raised their voices timidly, but they were promptly silenced by a tremendous growling from the dogs. Then, as usual, the sheep broke into "Four legs good, two legs bad!" and the momentary awkwardness was smoothed over. Finally Napoleon raised his trotter for silence and announced that he had already made all the arrangements. There would be no need for any of the animals to come in contact with human beings, which would clearly be most undesirable. He intended to take the whole burden upon his own shoulders. A Mr. Whymper, a solicitor living in Willingdon, had agreed to act as intermediary between Animal Farm and the outside world, and would visit the farm every Monday morning to receive his instructions. Napoleon ended his speech with his usual cry of "Long live Animal Farm!", and after the singing of "Beasts of England" the animals were dismissed.

Afterwards Squealer made a round of the farm and set the animals' minds at rest. He assured them that the resolution against engaging in trade and using money had never been passed, or even suggested. It was pure imagination, probably traceable in the beginning to lies circulated by Snowball. A few animals still felt faintly doubtful, but Squealer asked them shrewdly, "Are you certain that this is not something that you have dreamed, comrades? Have you any record of such a resolution? Is it written down anywhere?" And since it was certainly true that nothing of the kind existed in writing, the animals were satisfied that they had been mistaken.

Every Monday Mr. Whymper visited the farm as had been arranged. He was a sly-looking little man with side whiskers, a solicitor in a very small way of business, but sharp enough to have realised earlier than anyone else that Animal Farm would need a broker and that the commissions would be worth having. The animals watched his coming and going with a kind of dread, and avoided him as much as possible. Nevertheless, the sight of Napoleon, on all fours, delivering orders to Whymper, who stood on two legs, roused their pride and partly reconciled them to the new arrangement. Their relations with the human race were now not quite the same as they had been before. The human beings did not hate Animal Farm any less now that it was prospering; indeed, they hated it more than ever. Every human being held it as an article of faith that the farm would go bankrupt sooner or later, and, above all, that the windmill would be a failure. They would meet in the public-houses and prove to one another by means of diagrams that the windmill was bound to fall down, or that if it did stand up, then that it would never work. And yet, against their will, they had developed a certain respect for the efficiency with which the animals were managing their own affairs. One symptom of this was that they had begun to call Animal Farm by its proper name and ceased to pretend that it was called the Manor Farm. They had also dropped their championship of Jones, who had given up hope of getting his farm back and gone to live in another part of the county. Except through Whymper, there was as yet no contact between Animal Farm and the outside world, but there were constant rumours that Napoleon was about to enter into a definite business agreement either with Mr. Pilkington of Foxwood or with Mr. Frederick of Pinchfield—but never, it was noticed, with both simultaneously.

It was about this time that the pigs suddenly moved into

the farmhouse and took up their residence there. Again the animals seemed to remember that a resolution against this had been passed in the early days, and again Squealer was able to convince them that this was not the case. It was absolutely necessary, he said, that the pigs, who were the brains of the farm, should have a quiet place to work in. It was also more suited to the dignity of the Leader (for of late he had taken to speaking of Napoleon under the title of "Leader") to live in a house than in a mere sty. Nevertheless, some of the animals were disturbed when they heard that the pigs not only took their meals in the kitchen and used the drawing-room as a recreation room, but also slept in the beds. Boxer passed it off as usual with "Napoleon is always right!" but Clover, who thought she remembered a definite ruling against beds, went to the end of the barn and tried to puzzle out the Seven Commandments which were inscribed there. Finding herself unable to read more than individual letters, she fetched Muriel.

"Muriel," she said, "read me the Fourth Commandment. Does it not say something about never sleeping in a bed?"

With some difficulty Muriel spelt it out.

"It says, 'No animal shall sleep in a bed *with sheets*'," she announced finally.

Curiously enough, Clover had not remembered that the Fourth Commandment mentioned sheets; but as it was there on the wall, it must have done so. And Squealer, who happened to be passing at this moment, attended by two or three dogs, was able to put the whole matter in its proper perspective.

"You have heard then, comrades," he said, "that we pigs now sleep in the beds of the farmhouse? And why not? You did not suppose, surely, that there was ever a ruling against *beds*? A bed merely means a place to sleep in. A pile of straw in a stall is a bed, properly regarded. The rule was against *sheets*, which are a human invention. We have removed the sheets from the farmhouse beds, and sleep between blankets. And very comfortable beds they are too! But not more comfortable than we need, I can tell you, comrades, with all the brainwork we have to do nowadays. You would not rob us of our repose, would you, comrades? You would not have us too tired to carry out our duties? Surely none of you wishes to see Jones back?"

The animals reassured him on this point immediately, and no more was said about the pigs sleeping in the farmhouse beds. And when, some days afterwards, it was announced that from now on the pigs would get up an hour later in the mornings than the other animals, no complaint was made about that either.

By the autumn the animals were tired but happy. They had had a hard year, and after the sale of part of the hay and corn, the stores of food for the winter were none too plentiful, but the windmill compensated for everything. It was almost half built now. After the harvest there was a stretch of clear dry weather, and the animals toiled harder than ever, thinking it well worth while to plod to and fro all day with blocks of stone if by doing so they could raise the walls another foot. Boxer would even come out at nights and work for an hour or two on his own by the light of the harvest moon. In their spare moments the animals would walk round and round the half-finished mill, admiring the strength and perpendicularity of its walls and marvelling that they should ever have been able to build anything so imposing. Only old Benjamin refused to grow enthusiastic about the windmill, though, as usual, he would utter nothing beyond the cryptic remark that donkeys live a long time.

November came, with raging south-west winds. Building had to stop because it was now too wet to mix the cement. Finally there came a night when the gale was so violent that the farm buildings rocked on their foundations and several tiles were blown off the roof of the barn. The hens woke up squawking with terror because they had all dreamed simultaneously of hearing a gun go off in the distance. In the morning the animals came out of their stalls to find that the flagstaff had been blown down and an elm tree at the foot of the orchard had been plucked up like a radish. They had just noticed this when a cry of despair broke from every animal's throat. A terrible sight had met their eyes. The windmill was in ruins.

With one accord they dashed down to the spot. Napoleon, who seldom moved out of a walk, raced ahead of them all. Yes, there it lay, the fruit of all their struggles, levelled to its foundations, the stones they had broken and carried so laboriously scattered all around. Unable at first to speak, they stood gazing mournfully at the litter of fallen stone. Napoleon paced to and fro in silence, occasionally snuffing at the ground. His tail had grown rigid and twitched sharply from side to side, a sign in him of intense mental activity. Suddenly he halted as though his mind were made up.

"Comrades," he said quietly, "do you know who is responsible for this? Do you know the enemy who has come in the night and overthrown our windmill? SNOWBALL!" he suddenly roared in a voice of thunder. "Snowball has done this thing! In sheer malignity, thinking to set back our plans and avenge himself for his ignominious expulsion, this traitor has crept here under cover of night and destroyed our work of nearly a year. Comrades, here and now I pronounce the death sentence upon Snowball. 'Animal Hero, Second Class', and half a bushel of apples to any animal who brings him to justice. A full bushel to anyone who captures him alive!"

The animals were shocked beyond measure to learn that even Snowball could be guilty of such an action. There was a cry of indignation, and everyone began thinking out ways of catching Snowball if he should ever come back. Almost immediately the footprints of a pig were discovered in the grass at a little distance from the knoll. They could only be traced for a few yards, but appeared to lead to a hole in the hedge. Napoleon snuffed deeply at them and pronounced them to be Snowball's. He gave it as his opinion that Snowball had probably come from the direction of Foxwood Farm.

"No more delays, comrades!" cried Napoleon when the footprints had been examined. "There is work to be done. This very morning we begin rebuilding the windmill, and we will build all through the winter, rain or shine. We will teach this miserable traitor that he cannot undo our work so easily. Remember, comrades, there must be no alteration in our plans: they shall be carried out to the day. Forward, comrades! Long live the windmill! Long live Animal Farm!"

CHAPTER 7

It was a bitter winter. The stormy weather was followed by sleet and snow, and then by a hard frost which did not break till well into February. The animals carried on as best they could with the rebuilding of the windmill, well knowing that the outside world was watching them and that the envious human beings would rejoice and triumph if the mill were not finished on time.

Out of spite, the human beings pretended not to believe that it was Snowball who had destroyed the windmill: they said that it had fallen down because the walls were too thin. The animals knew that this was not the case. Still, it had been decided to build the walls three feet thick this time instead of eighteen inches as before, which meant collecting much larger quantities of stone. For a long time the quarry was full of snowdrifts and nothing could be done. Some progress was made in the dry frosty weather that followed, but it was cruel work, and the animals could not feel so hopeful about it as they had felt before. They were always cold, and usually hungry as well. Only Boxer and Clover never lost heart. Squealer made excellent speeches on the joy of service and the dignity of labour, but the other animals found more inspiration in Boxer's strength and his never-failing cry of "I will work harder!"

In January food fell short. The corn ration was drastically reduced, and it was announced that an extra potato ration would be issued to make up for it. Then it was discovered that the greater part of the potato crop had been frosted in the clamps, which had not been covered thickly enough. The potatoes had become soft and discoloured, and only a few were edible. For days at a time the animals had nothing to eat but chaff and mangels. Starvation seemed to stare them in the face.

It was vitally necessary to conceal this fact from the outside world. Emboldened by the collapse of the windmill, the human beings were inventing fresh lies about Animal Farm. Once again it was being put about that all the animals were dying of famine and disease, and that they were continually fighting among themselves and had resorted to cannibalism and infanticide. Napoleon was well aware of the bad results that might follow if the real facts of the food situation were known, and he decided to make use of Mr. Whymper to spread a contrary impression. Hitherto the animals had had little or no contact with Whymper on his weekly visits: now, however, a few selected animals, mostly sheep, were instructed to remark casually in his hearing that rations had been increased. In addition, Napoleon ordered the almost empty bins in the store-shed to be filled nearly to the brim with sand, which was then covered up with what remained of the grain and meal. On some suitable pretext Whymper was led through the store-shed and allowed to catch a glimpse of the bins. He was deceived, and continued to report to the outside world that there was no food shortage on Animal Farm.

Nevertheless, towards the end of January it became obvious that it would be necessary to procure some more grain from somewhere. In these days Napoleon rarely appeared in public, but spent all his time in the farmhouse, which was guarded at each door by fierce-looking dogs. When he did emerge, it was in a ceremonial manner, with an escort of six dogs who closely surrounded him and growled if anyone came too near. Frequently he did not even appear on Sunday mornings, but issued his orders through one of the other pigs, usually Squealer.

One Sunday morning Squealer announced that the hens, who had just come in to lay again, must surrender their eggs. Napoleon had accepted, through Whymper, a contract for four hundred eggs a week. The price of these would pay for enough grain and meal to keep the farm going till summer came on and conditions were easier.

When the hens heard this, they raised a terrible outcry. They had been warned earlier that this sacrifice might be necessary, but had not believed that it would really happen. They were just getting their clutches ready for the spring sitting, and they protested that to take the eggs away now was murder. For the first time since the expulsion of Jones, there was something resembling a rebellion. Led by three young Black Minorca pullets, the hens made a determined effort to thwart Napoleon's wishes. Their method was to fly up to the rafters and there lay their eggs, which smashed to pieces on the floor. Napoleon acted swiftly and ruthlessly. He ordered the hens' rations to be stopped, and decreed that any animal giving so much as a grain of corn to a hen should be punished by death. The dogs saw to it that these orders were carried out. For five days the hens held out, then they capitulated and went back to their nesting boxes. Nine hens had died in the meantime. Their bodies were buried in the orchard, and it was given out that they had died of coccidiosis. Whymper heard nothing of this affair, and the eggs were duly delivered, a grocer's van driving up to the farm once a week to take them away.

All this while no more had been seen of Snowball. He was rumoured to be hiding on one of the neighbouring farms, either Foxwood or Pinchfield. Napoleon was by this time on slightly better terms with the other farmers than before. It happened that there was in the yard a pile of timber which had been stacked there ten years earlier when a beech spinney was cleared. It was well seasoned, and Whymper had advised Napoleon to sell it; both Mr. Pilkington and Mr. Frederick were anxious to buy it. Napoleon was hesitating between the two, unable to make up his mind. It was noticed that whenever he seemed on the point of coming to an agreement with Frederick, Snowball was declared to be in hiding at Foxwood, while, when he inclined toward Pilkington, Snowball was said to be at Pinchfield.

Suddenly, early in the spring, an alarming thing was discovered. Snowball was secretly frequenting the farm by night! The animals were so disturbed that they could hardly sleep in their stalls. Every night, it was said, he came creeping in under cover of darkness and performed all kinds of mischief. He stole the corn, he upset the milk-pails, he broke the eggs, he trampled the seedbeds, he gnawed the bark off the fruit trees. Whenever anything went wrong it became usual to attribute it to Snowball. If a window was broken or a drain was blocked up, someone was certain to say that Snowball had come in the night and done it, and when the key of the store-shed was lost, the whole farm was convinced that Snowball had thrown it down the well. Curiously enough, they went on believing this even after the mislaid key was found under a sack of meal. The cows declared unanimously that Snowball crept into their stalls and milked them in their sleep. The rats, which had been troublesome that winter, were also said to be in league with Snowball.

Napoleon decreed that there should be a full investigation into Snowball's activities. With his dogs in attendance he set out and made a careful tour of inspection of the farm buildings, the other animals following at a respectful distance. At every few steps Napoleon stopped and snuffed the ground for traces of Snowball's footsteps, which, he said, he could detect by the smell. He snuffed in every corner, in the barn, in the cow-shed, in the henhouses, in the vegetable garden, and found traces of Snowball almost everywhere. He would put his snout to the ground, give several deep sniffs, and exclaim in a terrible voice, "Snowball! He has been here! I can smell him distinctly!" and at the word "Snowball" all the dogs let out blood-curdling growls and showed their side teeth.

The animals were thoroughly frightened. It seemed to them as though Snowball were some kind of invisible influence, pervading the air about them and menacing them with all kinds of dangers. In the evening Squealer called them together, and with an alarmed expression on his face told them that he had some serious news to report.

"Comrades!" cried Squealer, making little nervous skips, "a most terrible thing has been discovered. Snowball has sold himself to Frederick of Pinchfield Farm, who is even now plotting to attack us and take our farm away from us! Snowball is to act as his guide when the attack begins. But there is worse than that. We had thought that Snowball's rebellion was caused simply by his vanity and ambition. But we were wrong, comrades. Do you know what the real reason was? Snowball was in league with Jones from the very start! He was Jones's secret agent all the time. It has all been proved by documents which he left behind him and which we have only just discovered. To my mind this explains a great deal, comrades. Did we not see for ourselves how he attempted— fortunately without success—to get us defeated and destroyed at the Battle of the Cowshed?"

The animals were stupefied. This was a wickedness far outdoing Snowball's destruction of the windmill. But it was some minutes before they could fully take it in. They all remembered, or thought they remembered, how they had seen Snowball charging ahead of them at the Battle of the Cowshed, how he had rallied and encouraged them at every turn, and how he had not paused for an instant even when the pellets from Jones's gun had wounded his back. At first it was a little difficult to see how this fitted in with his being on Jones's side. Even Boxer, who seldom asked questions, was puzzled. He lay down, tucked his fore hoofs beneath him, shut his eyes, and with a hard effort managed to formulate his thoughts.

"I do not believe that," he said. "Snowball fought bravely at the Battle of the Cowshed. I saw him myself. Did we not give him 'Animal Hero, First Class', immediately afterwards?"

"That was our mistake, comrade. For we know now—it is all written down in the secret documents that we have found—that in reality he was trying to lure us to our doom."

"But he was wounded," said Boxer. "We all saw him running with blood."

"That was part of the arrangement!" cried Squealer. "Jones's shot only grazed him. I could show you this in his own writing, if you were able to read it. The plot was for Snowball, at the critical moment, to give the signal for flight and leave the field to the enemy. And he very nearly succeeded—I will even say, comrades, he *would* have succeeded if it had not been for our heroic Leader, Comrade Napoleon. Do you not remember how, just at the moment when Jones and his men had got inside the yard, Snowball suddenly turned and fled, and many animals followed him? And do you not remember, too, that it was just at that moment, when panic was spreading and all seemed lost, that Comrade Napoleon sprang forward with a cry of 'Death to Humanity!' and sank his teeth in Jones's leg? Surely you remember *that*, comrades?" exclaimed Squealer, frisking from side to side.

Now when Squealer described the scene so graphically, it seemed to the animals that they did remember it. At any rate, they remembered that at the critical moment of the battle Snowball had turned to flee. But Boxer was still a little uneasy.

"I do not believe that Snowball was a traitor at the beginning," he said finally. "What he has done since is different. But I believe that at the Battle of the Cowshed he was a good comrade."

"Our Leader, Comrade Napoleon," announced Squealer, speaking very slowly and firmly, "has stated categorically—categorically, comrade—that Snowball was Jones's agent from the very beginning—yes, and from long before the Rebellion was ever thought of."

"Ah, that is different!" said Boxer. "If Comrade Napoleon says it, it must be right."

"That is the true spirit, comrade!" cried Squealer, but it was noticed he cast a very ugly look at Boxer with his little twinkling eyes. He turned to go, then paused and added impressively: "I warn every animal on this farm to keep his eyes very wide open. For we have reason to think that some of Snowball's secret agents are lurking among us at this moment!"

Four days later, in the late afternoon, Napoleon ordered all the animals to assemble in the yard. When they were all gathered together, Napoleon emerged from the farmhouse, wearing both his medals (for he had recently awarded himself "Animal Hero, First Class", and "Animal Hero, Second Class"), with his nine huge dogs frisking round him and uttering growls that sent shivers down all the animals' spines. They all cowered silently in their places, seeming to know in advance that some terrible thing was about to happen.

Napoleon stood sternly surveying his audience; then he uttered a high-pitched whimper. Immediately the dogs bounded forward, seized four of the pigs by the ear and dragged them, squealing with pain and terror, to Napoleon's feet. The pigs' ears were bleeding, the dogs had tasted blood, and for a few moments they appeared to go quite mad. To the amazement of everybody, three of them flung themselves upon Boxer. Boxer saw them coming and put out his great hoof, caught a dog in mid-air, and pinned him to the ground. The dog shrieked for mercy and the other two fled with their tails between their legs. Boxer looked at Napoleon to know whether he should crush the dog to death or let it go. Napoleon appeared to change countenance, and sharply ordered Boxer to let the dog go, whereat Boxer lifted his hoof, and the dog slunk away, bruised and howling.

Presently the tumult died down. The four pigs waited, trembling, with guilt written on every line of their countenances. Napoleon now called upon them to confess their crimes. They were the same four pigs as had protested when Napoleon abolished the Sunday Meetings. Without any further prompting they confessed that they had been secretly in touch with Snowball ever since his expulsion, that they had collaborated with him in destroying the windmill, and that they had entered into an agreement with him to hand over Animal Farm to Mr. Frederick. They added that Snowball had privately admitted to them that he had been Jones's secret agent for years past. When they had finished their confession, the dogs promptly tore their throats out, and in a terrible voice Napoleon demanded whether any other animal had anything to confess.

The three hens who had been the ringleaders in the attempted rebellion over the eggs now came forward and stated that Snowball had appeared to them in a dream and incited them to disobey Napoleon's orders. They, too, were slaughtered. Then a goose came forward and confessed to having secreted six ears of corn during the last year's harvest and eaten them in the night. Then a sheep confessed to having urinated in the drinking pool—urged to do this, so she said, by Snowball—and two other sheep confessed to having murdered an old ram, an especially devoted follower of Napoleon, by chasing him round and round a bonfire when he was suffering from a cough. They were all slain on the spot. And so the tale of confessions and executions went on, until there was a pile of corpses lying before Napoleon's feet and the air was heavy with the smell of blood, which had been unknown there since the expulsion of Jones.

57

When it was all over, the remaining animals, except for the pigs and dogs, crept away in a body. They were shaken and miserable. They did not know which was more shocking— the treachery of the animals who had leagued themselves with Snowball, or the cruel retribution they had just witnessed. In the old days there had often been scenes of bloodshed equally terrible, but it seemed to all of them that it was far worse now that it was happening among themselves. Since Jones had left the farm, until today, no animal had killed another animal. Not even a rat had been killed. They had made their way on to the little knoll where the half-finished windmill stood, and with one accord they all lay down as though huddling together for warmth—Clover, Muriel, Benjamin, the cows, the sheep, and a whole flock of geese and hens— everyone, indeed, except the cat, who had suddenly disappeared just before Napoleon ordered the animals to assemble. For some time nobody spoke. Only Boxer remained on his feet. He fidgeted to and fro, swishing his long black tail against his sides and occasionally uttering a little whinny of surprise. Finally he said:

"I do not understand it. I would not have believed that such things could happen on our farm. It must be due to some fault in ourselves. The solution, as I see it, is to work harder. From now onwards I shall get up a full hour earlier in the mornings."

And he moved off at his lumbering trot and made for the quarry. Having got there, he collected two successive loads of stone and dragged them down to the windmill before retiring for the night.

The animals huddled about Clover, not speaking. The knoll where they were lying gave them a wide prospect across the countryside. Most of Animal Farm was within their view— the long pasture stretching down to the main road, the hayfield, the spinney, the drinking pool, the ploughed fields where the young wheat was thick and green, and the red roofs of the farm buildings with the smoke curling from the chimneys. It was a clear spring evening. The grass and the bursting hedges were gilded by the level rays of the sun. Never had the farm—and with a kind of surprise they remembered that it was their own farm, every inch of it their own property— appeared to the animals so desirable a place. As Clover looked down the hillside her eyes filled with tears. If she could have spoken her thoughts, it would have been to say that this was not what they had aimed at when they had set themselves years ago to work for the overthrow of the human race. These scenes of terror and slaughter were not what they had looked forward to on that night when old Major first stirred them to rebellion. If she herself had had any picture of the future, it had been of a society of animals set free from hunger and the whip, all equal, each working according to his capacity, the strong protecting the weak, as she had protected the lost brood of ducklings with her foreleg on the night of Major's speech. Instead—she did not know why—they had come to a time when no one dared speak his mind, when fierce, growling dogs roamed everywhere, and when you had to watch your comrades torn to pieces after confessing to shocking crimes. There was no thought of rebellion or disobedience in her mind. She knew that, even as things were, they were far better off than they had been in the days of Jones, and that before all else it was needful to prevent the return of the human beings. Whatever happened she would remain faithful, work hard, carry out the orders that were given to her, and accept the leadership of Napoleon. But still, it was not for this that she and all the other animals had hoped and toiled. It was not for this that they had built the windmill and faced the bullets of Jones's gun. Such were her thoughts, though she lacked the words to express them.

At last, feeling this to be in some way a substitute for the words she was unable to find, she began to sing "Beasts of England". The other animals sitting round her took it up, and they sang it three times over—very tunefully, but slowly and mournfully, in a way they had never sung it before.

They had just finished singing it for the third time when Squealer, attended by two dogs, approached them with the air of having something important to say. He announced that, by a special decree of Comrade Napoleon, "Beasts of England" had been abolished. From now onwards it was forbidden to sing it.

The animals were taken aback.

"Why?" cried Muriel.

"It's no longer needed, comrade," said Squealer stiffly. "'Beasts of England' was the song of the Rebellion. But the Rebellion is now completed. The execution of the traitors this afternoon was the final act. The enemy both external and internal has been defeated. In "Beasts of England" we expressed our longing for a better society in days to come. But that society has now been established. Clearly this song has no longer any purpose."

Frightened though they were, some of the animals might possibly have protested, but at this moment the sheep set up their usual bleating of "Four legs good, two legs bad", which went on for several minutes and put an end to the discussion.

So "Beasts of England" was heard no more. In its place Minimus, the poet, had composed another song which began:

Animal Farm, Animal Farm,
    Never through me shalt thou come to harm!

and this was sung every Sunday morning after the hoisting of the flag. But somehow neither the words nor the tune ever seemed to the animals to come up to "Beasts of England".

CHAPTER 8

A few days later, when the terror caused by the executions had died down, some of the animals remembered—or thought they remembered—that the Sixth Commandment decreed "No animal shall kill any other animal". And though no one cared to mention it in the hearing of the pigs or the dogs, it was felt that the killings which had taken place did not square with this. Clover asked Benjamin to read her the Sixth Commandment, and when Benjamin, as usual, said that he refused to meddle in such matters, she fetched Muriel. Muriel read the Commandment for her. It ran: "No animal shall kill any other animal *without cause*". Somehow or other, the last two words had slipped out of the animals' memory. But they saw now that the Commandment had not been violated; for clearly there was good reason for killing the traitors who had leagued themselves with Snowball.

Throughout the year the animals worked even harder than they had worked in the previous year. To rebuild the windmill, with walls twice as thick as before, and to finish it by the appointed date, together with the regular work of the farm, was a tremendous labour. There were times when it seemed to the animals that they worked longer hours and fed no better than they had done in Jones's day. On Sunday mornings Squealer, holding down a long strip of paper with his trotter, would read out to them lists of figures proving that the production of every class of foodstuff had increased by two hundred per cent, three hundred per cent, or five hundred per cent, as the case might be. The animals saw no reason to disbelieve him, especially as they could no longer remember very clearly what conditions had been like before the Rebellion. All the same, there were days when they felt that they would sooner have had less figures and more food.

All orders were now issued through Squealer or one of the other pigs. Napoleon himself was not seen in public as often as once in a fortnight. When he did appear, he was attended not only by his retinue of dogs but by a black cockerel who marched in front of him and acted as a kind of trumpeter, letting out a loud "cock-a-doodle-doo" before Napoleon spoke. Even in the farmhouse, it was said, Napoleon inhabited separate apartments from the others. He took his meals alone, with two dogs to wait upon him, and always ate from the Crown Derby dinner service which had been in the glass cupboard in the drawing-room. It was also announced that the gun would be fired every year on Napoleon's birthday, as well as on the other two anniversaries.

Napoleon was now never spoken of simply as "Napoleon". He was always referred to in formal style as "our Leader, Comrade Napoleon", and the pigs liked to invent for him such titles as Father of All Animals, Terror of Mankind, Protector of the Sheep-fold, Ducklings' Friend, and the like. In his speeches, Squealer would talk with the tears rolling down his cheeks of Napoleon's wisdom, the goodness of his heart, and the deep love he bore to all animals everywhere, even and especially the unhappy animals who still lived in ignorance and slavery on other farms. It had become usual to give Napoleon the credit for every successful achievement and every stroke of good fortune. You would often hear one hen remark to another, "Under the guidance of our Leader,

Comrade Napoleon, I have laid five eggs in six days"; or two cows, enjoying a drink at the pool, would exclaim, "Thanks to the leadership of Comrade Napoleon, how excellent this water tastes!" The general feeling on the farm was well expressed in a poem entitled 'Comrade Napoleon', which was composed by Minimus and which ran as follows:

> Friend of fatherless!
> Fountain of happiness!
> Lord of the swill-bucket! Oh, how my soul is on
> Fire when I gaze at thy
> Calm and commanding eye,
> Like the sun in the sky,
> Comrade Napoleon!

> Thou are the giver of
> All that thy creatures love,
> Full belly twice a day, clean straw to roll upon;
> Every beast great or small
> Sleeps at peace in his stall,
> Thou watchest over all,
> Comrade Napoleon!

> Had I a sucking-pig,
> Ere he had grown as big
> Even as a pint bottle or as a rolling-pin,
> He should have learned to be
> Faithful and true to thee,
> Yes, his first squeak should be
> "Comrade Napoleon!"

Napoleon approved of this poem and caused it to be inscribed on the wall of the big barn, at the opposite end from the Seven Commandments. It was surmounted by a portrait of Napoleon, in profile, executed by Squealer in white paint.

Meanwhile, through the agency of Whymper, Napoleon was engaged in complicated negotiations with Frederick and Pilkington. The pile of timber was still unsold. Of the two, Frederick was the more anxious to get hold of it, but he would not offer a reasonable price. At the same time there were renewed rumours that Frederick and his men were plotting to attack Animal Farm and to destroy the windmill, the building of which had aroused furious jealousy in him. Snowball was known to be still skulking on Pinchfield Farm. In the middle of the summer the animals were alarmed to hear that three hens had come forward and confessed that, inspired by Snowball, they had entered into a plot to murder Napoleon. They were executed immediately, and fresh precautions for Napoleon's safety were taken. Four dogs guarded his bed at night, one at each corner, and a young pig named Pinkeye was given the task of tasting all his food before he ate it, lest it should be poisoned.

At about the same time it was given out that Napoleon had arranged to sell the pile of timber to Mr. Pilkington; he was also going to enter into a regular agreement for the exchange of certain products between Animal Farm and Foxwood. The relations between Napoleon and Pilkington, though they were only conducted through Whymper, were now almost friendly. The animals distrusted Pilkington, as a human being, but greatly preferred him to Frederick, whom they both feared and hated. As the summer wore on, and the windmill neared completion, the rumours of an impending treacherous attack grew stronger and stronger. Frederick, it was said, intended to bring against them twenty men all armed with guns, and he had already bribed the magistrates and police, so that if he could once get hold of the title-deeds of Animal Farm they would ask no questions. Moreover, terrible stories were leaking out from Pinchfield about the cruelties that Frederick practised upon his animals. He had flogged an old horse to death, he starved his cows, he had killed a dog by throwing it into the furnace, he amused himself in the evenings by making cocks fight with splinters of razor-blade tied to their spurs. The animals' blood boiled with rage when they heard of these things being done to their comrades, and sometimes they clamoured to be allowed to go out in a body and attack Pinchfield Farm, drive out the humans, and set the animals free. But Squealer counselled them to avoid rash actions and trust in Comrade Napoleon's strategy.

Nevertheless, feeling against Frederick continued to run high. One Sunday morning Napoleon appeared in the barn and explained that he had never at any time contemplated selling the pile of timber to Frederick; he considered it beneath his dignity, he said, to have dealings with scoundrels of that description. The pigeons who were still sent out to spread tidings of the Rebellion were forbidden to set foot anywhere on Foxwood, and were also ordered to drop their former slogan of "Death to Humanity" in favour of "Death to Frederick". In the late summer yet another of Snowball's machinations was laid bare. The wheat crop was full of weeds, and it was discovered that on one of his nocturnal visits Snowball had mixed weed seeds with the seed corn. A gander who had been privy to the plot had confessed his guilt to Squealer and immediately committed suicide by swallowing deadly night-shade berries. The animals now also learned that Snowball had never—as many of them had believed hitherto—received the order of "Animal Hero First Class". This was merely a legend which had been spread some time after the Battle of the Cowshed by Snowball himself. So far from being deco-rated, he had been censured for showing cowardice in the battle. Once again some of the animals heard this with a certain bewilderment, but Squealer was soon able to convince them that their memories had been at fault.

In the autumn, by a tremendous, exhausting effort—for the harvest had to be gathered at almost the same time—the windmill was finished. The machinery had still to be installed, and Whymper was negotiating the purchase of it, but the structure was completed. In the teeth of every difficulty, in spite of inexperience, of primitive implements, of bad luck and of Snowball's treachery, the work had been finished punctually to the very day! Tired out but proud, the animals walked round and round their masterpiece, which appeared even more beautiful in their eyes than when it had been built the first time. Moreover, the walls were twice as thick as before. Nothing short of explosives would lay them low this time! And when they thought of how they had laboured, what discouragements they had overcome, and the enormous difference that would be made in their lives when the sails were turning and the dynamos running—when they thought of all this, their tiredness forsook them and they gambolled round and round the windmill, uttering cries of triumph. Napoleon himself, attended by his dogs and his cockerel, came down to inspect the completed work; he personally congratulated the animals on their achievement, and announced that the mill would be named Napoleon Mill.

Two days later the animals were called together for a special meeting in the barn. They were struck dumb with surprise when Napoleon announced that he had sold the pile of timber to Frederick. Tomorrow Frederick's wagons would arrive and begin carting it away. Throughout the whole period of his seeming friendship with Pilkington, Napoleon had really been in secret agreement with Frederick.

All relations with Foxwood had been broken off; insulting messages had been sent to Pilkington. The pigeons had been told to avoid Pinchfield Farm and to alter their slogan from "Death to Frederick" to "Death to Pilkington". At the same time Napoleon assured the animals that the stories of an impending attack on Animal Farm were completely untrue, and that the tales about Frederick's cruelty to his own animals had been greatly exaggerated. All these rumours had probably originated with Snowball and his agents. It now appeared that

Snowball was not, after all, hiding on Pinchfield Farm, and in fact had never been there in his life: he was living—in considerable luxury, so it was said—at Foxwood, and had in reality been a pensioner of Pilkington for years past.

The pigs were in ecstasies over Napoleon's cunning. By seeming to be friendly with Pilkington he had forced Frederick to raise his price by twelve pounds. But the superior quality of Napoleon's mind, said Squealer, was shown in the fact that he trusted nobody, not even Frederick. Frederick had wanted to pay for the timber with something called a cheque, which, it seemed, was a piece of paper with a promise to pay written upon it. But Napoleon was too clever for him. He had demanded payment in real five-pound notes, which were to be handed over before the timber was removed. Already Frederick had paid up; and the sum he had paid was just enough to buy the machinery for the windmill.

Meanwhile the timber was being carted away at high speed. When it was all gone, another special meeting was held in the barn for the animals to inspect Frederick's banknotes. Smiling beatifically, and wearing both his decorations, Napoleon reposed on a bed of straw on the platform, with the money at his side, neatly piled on a china dish from the farmhouse kitchen. The animals filed slowly past, and each gazed his fill. And Boxer put out his nose to sniff at the banknotes, and the flimsy white things stirred and rustled in his breath.

Three days later there was a terrible hullabaloo. Whymper, his face deadly pale, came racing up the path on his bicycle, flung it down in the yard and rushed straight into the farmhouse. The next moment a choking roar of rage sounded from Napoleon's apartments. The news of what had happened sped round the farm like wildfire. The banknotes were forgeries! Frederick had got the timber for nothing!

Napoleon called the animals together immediately and in a terrible voice pronounced the death sentence upon

Frederick. When captured, he said, Frederick should be boiled alive. At the same time he warned them that after this treacherous deed the worst was to be expected. Frederick and his men might make their long-expected attack at any moment. Sentinels were placed at all the approaches to the farm. In addition, four pigeons were sent to Foxwood with a conciliatory message, which it was hoped might re-establish good relations with Pilkington.

The very next morning the attack came. The animals were at breakfast when the look-outs came racing in with the news that Frederick and his followers had already come through the five-barred gate. Boldly enough the animals sallied forth to meet them, but this time they did not have the easy victory that they had had in the Battle of the Cowshed. There were fifteen men, with half a dozen guns between them, and they opened fire as soon as they got within fifty yards. The animals could not face the terrible explosions and the stinging pellets, and in spite of the efforts of Napoleon and Boxer to rally them, they were soon driven back. A number of them were already wounded. They took refuge in the farm buildings and peeped cautiously out from chinks and knotholes. The whole of the big pasture, including the windmill, was in the hands of the enemy. For the moment even Napoleon seemed at a loss. He paced up and down without a word, his tail rigid and twitching. Wistful glances were sent in the direction of Foxwood. If Pilkington and his men would help them, the day might yet be won. But at this moment the four pigeons, who had been sent out on the day before, returned, one of them bearing a scrap of paper from Pilkington. On it was pencilled the words: "Serves you right".

Meanwhile Frederick and his men had halted about the windmill. The animals watched them, and a murmur of dismay went round. Two of the men had produced a crowbar and a sledge hammer. They were going to knock the windmill down.

"Impossible!" cried Napoleon. "We have built the walls far too thick for that. They could not knock it down in a week. Courage, comrades!"

But Benjamin was watching the movements of the men intently. The two with the hammer and the crowbar were drilling a hole near the base of the windmill. Slowly, and with an air almost of amusement, Benjamin nodded his long muzzle.

"I thought so," he said. "Do you not see what they are doing? In another moment they are going to pack blasting powder into that hole."

Terrified, the animals waited. It was impossible now to venture out of the shelter of the buildings. After a few minutes the men were seen to be running in all directions. Then there was a deafening roar. The pigeons swirled into the air, and all the animals, except Napoleon, flung themselves flat on their bellies and hid their faces. When they got up again, a huge cloud of black smoke was hanging where the windmill had been. Slowly the breeze drifted it away. The windmill had ceased to exist!

At this sight the animals' courage returned to them. The fear and despair they had felt a moment earlier were drowned in their rage against this vile, contemptible act. A mighty cry for vengeance went up, and without waiting for further orders they charged forth in a body and made straight for the enemy. This time they did not heed the cruel pellets that swept over them like hail. It was a savage, bitter battle. The men fired again and again, and, when the animals got to close quarters, lashed out with their sticks and their heavy boots. A cow, three sheep, and two geese were killed, and nearly everyone was wounded. Even Napoleon, who was directing operations from the rear, had the tip of his tail chipped by a pellet. But the men did not go unscathed either. Three of them had their heads broken by blows from Boxer's hoofs; another was gored in the belly by a cow's horn; another had his trousers nearly torn off by Jessie and Bluebell. And when the nine dogs of Napoleon's own bodyguard, whom he had instructed to make a detour under cover of the hedge, suddenly appeared on the men's flank, baying ferociously, panic overtook them. They saw that they were in danger of being surrounded. Frederick shouted to his men to get out while the going was good, and the next moment the cowardly enemy was running for dear life. The animals chased them right down to the bottom of the field, and got in some last kicks at them as they forced their way through the thorn hedge.

They had won, but they were weary and bleeding. Slowly they began to limp back towards the farm. The sight of their dead comrades stretched upon the grass moved some of them to tears. And for a little while they halted in sorrowful silence at the place where the windmill had once stood. Yes, it was gone; almost the last trace of their labour was gone! Even the foundations were partially destroyed. And in rebuilding it they could not this time, as before, make use of the fallen stones. This time the stones had vanished too. The force of the explosion had flung them to distances of hundreds of yards. It was as though the windmill had never been.

As they approached the farm Squealer, who had unaccountably been absent during the fighting, came skipping towards them, whisking his tail and beaming with satisfaction. And the animals heard, from the direction of the farm buildings, the solemn booming of a gun.

"What is that gun firing for?" said Boxer.

"To celebrate our victory!" cried Squealer.

"What victory?" said Boxer. His knees were bleeding, he had lost a shoe and split his hoof, and a dozen pellets had lodged themselves in his hind leg.

"What victory, comrade? Have we not driven the enemy off our soil—the sacred soil of Animal Farm?"

"But they have destroyed the windmill. And we had worked on it for two years!"

"What matter? We will build another windmill. We will build six windmills if we feel like it. You do not appreciate, comrade, the mighty thing that we have done. The enemy was in occupation of this very ground that we stand upon. And now—thanks to the leadership of Comrade Napoleon—we have won every inch of it back again!"

"Then we have won back what we had before," said Boxer.

"That is our victory," said Squealer.

They limped into the yard. The pellets under the skin of Boxer's leg smarted painfully. He saw ahead of him the heavy labour of rebuilding the windmill from the foundations, and already in imagination he braced himself for the task. But for the first time it occurred to him that he was eleven years old and that perhaps his great muscles were not quite what they had once been.

But when the animals saw the green flag flying, and heard the gun firing again—seven times it was fired in all—and heard the speech that Napoleon made, congratulating them on their conduct, it did seem to them after all that they had won a great victory. The animals slain in the battle were given a solemn funeral. Boxer and Clover pulled the wagon which served as a hearse, and Napoleon himself walked at the head of the procession. Two whole days were given over to celebrations. There were songs, speeches, and more firing of the gun, and a special gift of an apple was bestowed on every animal, with two ounces of corn for each bird and three biscuits for each dog. It was announced that the battle would be called the Battle of the Windmill, and that Napoleon had created a new decoration, the Order of the Green Banner, which he had conferred upon himself. In the general rejoicings the unfortunate affair of the banknotes was forgotten.

It was a few days later than this that the pigs came upon a case of whisky in the cellars of the farmhouse. It had been overlooked at the time when the house was first occupied.

That night there came from the farmhouse the sound of loud singing, in which, to everyone's surprise, the strains of "Beasts of England" were mixed up. At about half-past nine Napoleon, wearing an old bowler hat of Mr. Jones's, was distinctly seen to emerge from the back door, gallop rapidly round the yard, and disappear indoors again. But in the morning a deep silence hung over the farmhouse. Not a pig appeared to be stirring. It was nearly nine o'clock when Squealer made his appearance, walking slowly and dejectedly, his eyes dull, his tail hanging limply behind him, and with every appearance of being seriously ill. He called the animals together and told them that he had a terrible piece of news to impart. Comrade Napoleon was dying!

A cry of lamentation went up. Straw was laid down outside the doors of the farmhouse, and the animals walked on tiptoe. With tears in their eyes they asked one another what they should do if their Leader were taken away from them. A rumour went round that Snowball had after all contrived to introduce poison into Napoleon's food. At eleven o'clock Squealer came out to make another announcement. As his last act upon earth, Comrade Napoleon had pronounced a solemn decree: the drinking of alcohol was to be punished by death.

By the evening, however, Napoleon appeared to be somewhat better, and the following morning Squealer was able to tell them that he was well on the way to recovery. By the evening of that day Napoleon was back at work, and on the next day it was learned that he had instructed Whymper to purchase in Willingdon some booklets on brewing and distilling. A week later Napoleon gave orders that the small paddock beyond the orchard, which it had previously been intended to set aside as a grazing-ground for animals who were past work, was to be ploughed up. It was given out that the pasture was exhausted and needed reseeding; but it soon became known that Napoleon intended to sow it with barley.

About this time there occurred a strange incident which hardly anyone was able to understand. One night at about twelve o'clock there was a loud crash in the yard, and the animals rushed out of their stalls. It was a moonlit night. At the foot of the end wall of the big barn, where the Seven Commandments were written, there lay a ladder broken in two pieces. Squealer, temporarily stunned, was sprawling beside it, and near at hand there lay a lantern, a paint-brush, and an overturned pot of white paint. The dogs immediately made a ring round Squealer, and escorted him back to the farmhouse as soon as he was able to walk. None of the animals could form any idea as to what this meant, except old Benjamin, who nodded his muzzle with a knowing air, and seemed to understand, but would say nothing.

But a few days later Muriel, reading over the Seven Commandments to herself, noticed that there was yet another of them which the animals had remembered wrong. They had thought the Fifth Commandment was "No animal shall drink alcohol", but there were two words that they had forgotten. Actually the Commandment read: "No animal shall drink alcohol *to excess*".

CHAPTER 9

Boxer's split hoof was a long time in healing. They had started the rebuilding of the windmill the day after the victory celebrations were ended. Boxer refused to take even a day off work, and made it a point of honour not to let it be seen that he was in pain. In the evenings he would admit privately to Clover that the hoof troubled him a great deal. Clover treated the hoof with poultices of herbs which she prepared by chewing them, and both she and Benjamin urged Boxer to work less hard. "A horse's lungs do not last for ever," she said to him. But Boxer would not listen. He had, he said, only one real ambition left—to see the windmill well under way before he reached the age for retirement.

At the beginning, when the laws of Animal Farm were first formulated, the retiring age had been fixed for horses and pigs at twelve, for cows at fourteen, for dogs at nine, for sheep at seven, and for hens and geese at five. Liberal old-age pensions had been agreed upon. As yet no animal had actually retired on pension, but of late the subject had been discussed more and more. Now that the small field beyond the orchard had been set aside for barley, it was rumoured that a corner of the large pasture was to be fenced off and turned into a grazing-ground for superannuated animals. For a horse, it was said, the pension would be five pounds of corn a day and, in winter, fifteen pounds of hay, with a carrot or possibly an apple on public holidays. Boxer's twelfth birthday was due in the late summer of the following year.

Meanwhile life was hard. The winter was as cold as the last one had been, and food was even shorter. Once again all rations were reduced, except those of the pigs and the dogs. A too rigid equality in rations, Squealer explained, would have been contrary to the principles of Animalism. In any case he had no difficulty in proving to the other animals that they were *not* in reality short of food, whatever the appearances might be. For the time being, certainly, it had been found necessary to make a readjustment of rations (Squealer always spoke of it as a "readjustment", never as a "reduction"), but in comparison with the days of Jones, the improvement was enormous. Reading out the figures in a shrill, rapid voice, he proved to them in detail that they had more oats, more hay, more turnips than they had had in Jones's day, that they worked shorter hours, that their drinking water was of better quality, that they lived longer, that a larger proportion of their young ones survived infancy, and that they had more straw in their stalls and suffered less from fleas. The animals believed every word of it. Truth to tell, Jones and all he stood for had almost faded out of their memories. They knew that life nowadays was harsh and bare, that they were often hungry and often cold, and that they were usually working when they were not asleep. But doubtless it had been worse in the old days. They were glad to believe so. Besides, in those days they had been slaves and now they were free, and that made all the difference, as Squealer did not fail to point out.

There were many more mouths to feed now. In the autumn the four sows had all littered about simultaneously, producing thirty-one young pigs between them. The young pigs were piebald, and as Napoleon was the only boar on the farm, it was possible to guess at their parentage. It was announced that later, when bricks and timber had been purchased, a schoolroom would be built in the farmhouse garden. For the time being, the young pigs were given their instruction by Napoleon himself in the farmhouse kitchen. They took their exercise in the garden, and were discouraged from playing with the other young animals. About this time, too, it was laid down as a rule that when a pig and any other animal met on the path, the other animal must stand aside: and also that all pigs, of whatever degree, were to have the privilege of wearing green ribbons on their tails on Sundays.

The farm had had a fairly successful year, but was still short of money. There were the bricks, sand, and lime for the schoolroom to be purchased, and it would also be necessary to begin saving up again for the machinery for the windmill. Then there were lamp oil and candles for the house, sugar for Napoleon's own table (he forbade this to the other pigs, on the ground that it made them fat), and all the usual replacements such as tools, nails, string, coal, wire, scrap-iron, and dog biscuits. A stump of hay and part of the potato crop were sold off, and the contract for eggs was increased to six hundred a week, so that that year the hens barely hatched enough chicks to keep their numbers at the same level. Rations, reduced in December, were reduced again in February, and lanterns in the stalls were forbidden, to save oil. But the pigs seemed comfortable enough, and in fact were putting on weight if anything. One afternoon in late February a warm, rich, appetising scent, such as the animals had never smelt before, wafted itself across the yard from the little brew-house, which had been disused in Jones's time, and which stood beyond the kitchen. Someone said it was the smell of cooking barley. The animals sniffed the air hungrily and wondered whether a warm mash was being prepared for their supper. But no warm mash appeared, and on the following Sunday it was announced that from now onwards all barley would be reserved for the pigs. The field beyond the orchard had already been sown with barley. And the news soon leaked out that every pig was now receiving a ration of a pint of beer daily, with half a gallon for Napoleon himself, which was always served to him in the Crown Derby soup tureen.

But if there were hardships to be borne, they were partly offset by the fact that life nowadays had a greater dignity than it had had before. There were more songs, more speeches, more processions. Napoleon had commanded that once a week there should be held something called a Spontaneous Demonstration, the object of which was to celebrate the struggles and triumphs of Animal Farm. At the appointed time the animals would leave their work and march round the precincts of the farm in military formation, with the pigs leading, then the horses, then the cows, then the sheep, and then the poultry. The dogs flanked the procession and at the head of all marched Napoleon's black cockerel. Boxer and Clover always carried between them a green banner marked with the hoof and the horn and the caption, "Long live Comrade Napoleon!" Afterwards there were recitations of poems composed in Napoleon's honour, and a speech by Squealer giving particulars of the latest increases in the production of foodstuffs, and on occasion a shot was fired from the gun. The sheep were the greatest devotees of the Spontaneous Demonstration, and if anyone complained (as a few animals sometimes did, when no pigs or dogs were near) that they wasted time and meant a lot of standing about in the cold, the sheep were sure to silence him with a tremendous bleating of "Four legs good, two legs bad!" But by and large the animals enjoyed these celebrations. They found it comforting to be reminded that, after all, they were truly their own masters and that the work they did was for their own benefit. So that, what with the songs, the processions, Squealer's lists of figures, the thunder of the gun, the crowing of the cockerel, and the fluttering of the flag, they were able to forget that their bellies were empty, at least part of the time.

In April, Animal Farm was proclaimed a Republic, and it became necessary to elect a President. There was only one candidate, Napoleon, who was elected unanimously. On the same day it was given out that fresh documents had been discovered which revealed further details about Snowball's complicity with Jones. It now appeared that Snowball had not, as the animals had previously imagined, merely attempted to lose the Battle of the Cowshed by means of a stratagem, but had been openly fighting on Jones's side. In fact, it was he who had actually been the leader of the human forces, and had charged into battle with the words "Long live Humanity!" on his lips. The wounds on Snowball's back, which a few of the animals still remembered to have seen, had been inflicted by Napoleon's teeth.

In the middle of the summer Moses the raven suddenly reappeared on the farm, after an absence of several years. He was quite unchanged, still did no work, and talked in the same strain as ever about Sugarcandy Mountain. He would perch on a stump, flap his black wings, and talk by the hour to anyone who would listen. "Up there, comrades," he would say solemnly, pointing to the sky with his large beak—"up there, just on the other side of that dark cloud that you can see—there it lies, Sugarcandy Mountain, that happy country where we poor animals shall rest for ever from our labours!" He even claimed to have been there on one of his higher flights, and to have seen the everlasting fields of clover and the linseed cake and lump sugar growing on the hedges. Many of the animals believed him. Their lives now, they reasoned, were hungry and laborious; was it not right and just that a better world should exist somewhere else? A thing that was difficult to determine was the attitude of the pigs towards Moses. They all declared contemptuously that his stories about Sugarcandy Mountain were lies, and yet they allowed him to remain on the farm, not working, with an allowance of a gill of beer a day.

After his hoof had healed up, Boxer worked harder than ever. Indeed, all the animals worked like slaves that year. Apart from the regular work of the farm, and the rebuilding of the windmill, there was the schoolhouse for the young pigs, which was started in March. Sometimes the long hours on insufficient food were hard to bear, but Boxer never faltered. In nothing that he said or did was there any sign that his strength was not what it had been. It was only his appearance that was a little altered; his hide was less shiny than it had used to be, and his great haunches seemed to have shrunken. The others said, "Boxer will pick up when the spring grass comes on"; but the spring came and Boxer grew no fatter. Sometimes on the slope leading to the top of the quarry, when he braced his muscles against the weight of some vast boulder, it seemed that nothing kept him on his feet except the will to continue. At such times his lips were seen to form the words, "I will work harder"; he had no voice left. Once again Clover and Benjamin warned him to take care of his health, but Boxer paid no attention. His twelfth birthday was approaching. He did not care what happened so long as a good store of stone was accumulated before he went on pension.

Late one evening in the summer, a sudden rumour ran round the farm that something had happened to Boxer. He had gone out alone to drag a load of stone down to the windmill. And sure enough, the rumour was true. A few minutes later two pigeons came racing in with the news: "Boxer has fallen! He is lying on his side and can't get up!"

About half the animals on the farm rushed out to the knoll where the windmill stood. There lay Boxer, between the shafts of the cart, his neck stretched out, unable even to raise his head. His eyes were glazed, his sides matted with sweat. A thin stream of blood had trickled out of his mouth. Clover dropped to her knees at his side.

"Boxer!" she cried, "how are you?"

"It is my lung," said Boxer in a weak voice. "It does not matter. I think you will be able to finish the windmill without me. There is a pretty good store of stone accumulated. I had only another month to go in any case. To tell you the truth, I had been looking forward to my retirement. And perhaps, as Benjamin is growing old too, they will let him retire at the same time and be a companion to me."

"We must get help at once," said Clover. "Run, somebody, and tell Squealer what has happened."

All the other animals immediately raced back to the farmhouse to give Squealer the news. Only Clover remained, and Benjamin, who lay down at Boxer's side, and, without speaking, kept the flies off him with his long tail. After about a quarter of an hour Squealer appeared, full of sympathy and concern. He said that Comrade Napoleon had learned with the very deepest distress of this misfortune to one of the most loyal workers on the farm, and was already making arrangements to send Boxer to be treated in the hospital at Willingdon. The animals felt a little uneasy at this. Except for Mollie and Snowball, no other animal had ever left the farm, and they did not like to think of their sick comrade in the hands of human beings. However, Squealer easily convinced them that the veterinary surgeon in Willingdon could treat Boxer's case more satisfactorily than could be done on the farm. And about half an hour later, when Boxer had somewhat recovered, he was with difficulty got on to his feet, and managed to limp back to his stall, where Clover and Benjamin had prepared a good bed of straw for him.

For the next two days Boxer remained in his stall. The pigs had sent out a large bottle of pink medicine which they had found in the medicine chest in the bathroom, and Clover administered it to Boxer twice a day after meals. In the evenings she lay in his stall and talked to him, while Benjamin kept the flies off him. Boxer professed not to be sorry for what had happened. If he made a good recovery, he might expect to live another three years, and he looked forward to the peaceful days that he would spend in the corner of the big pasture. It would be the first time that he had had leisure to study and improve his mind. He intended, he said, to devote the rest of his life to learning the remaining twenty-two letters of the alphabet.

However, Benjamin and Clover could only be with Boxer after working hours, and it was in the middle of the day when the van came to take him away. The animals were all at work weeding turnips under the supervision of a pig, when they were astonished to see Benjamin come galloping from the direction of the farm buildings, braying at the top of his voice. It was the first time that they had ever seen Benjamin excited—indeed, it was the first time that anyone had ever seen him gallop. "Quick, quick!" he shouted. "Come at once! They're taking Boxer away!" Without waiting for orders from the pig, the animals broke off work and raced back to the farm buildings. Sure enough, there in the yard was a large closed van, drawn by two horses, with lettering on its side and a sly-looking man in a low-crowned bowler hat sitting on the driver's seat. And Boxer's stall was empty.

The animals crowded round the van. "Good-bye, Boxer!" they chorused, "good-bye!"

"Fools! Fools!" shouted Benjamin, prancing round them and stamping the earth with his small hoofs. "Fools! Do you not see what is written on the side of that van?"

That gave the animals pause, and there was a hush. Muriel began to spell out the words. But Benjamin pushed her aside and in the midst of a deadly silence he read:

" 'Alfred Simmonds, Horse Slaughterer and Glue Boiler, Willingdon. Dealer in Hides and Bone-Meal. Kennels Supplied.' Do you not understand what that means? They are taking Boxer to the knacker's!"

A cry of horror burst from all the animals. At this moment the man on the box whipped up his horses and the van moved out of the yard at a smart trot. All the animals followed, crying out at the tops of their voices. Clover forced her way to the front. The van began to gather speed. Clover tried to stir her stout limbs to a gallop, and achieved a canter. "Boxer!" she cried. "Boxer! Boxer! Boxer!" And just at this moment, as though he had heard the uproar outside, Boxer's face, with the white stripe down his nose, appeared at the small window at the back of the van.

"Boxer!" cried Clover in a terrible voice. "Boxer! Get out! Get out quickly! They're taking you to your death!"

All the animals took up the cry of "Get out, Boxer, get out!" But the van was already gathering speed and drawing away from them. It was uncertain whether Boxer had understood what Clover had said. But a moment later his face disappeared from the window and there was the sound of a tremendous drumming of hoofs inside the van. He was trying to kick his way out. The time had been when a few kicks from Boxer's hoofs would have smashed the van to matchwood. But alas! his strength had left him; and in a few moments the sound of drumming hoofs grew fainter and died away. In desperation the animals began appealing to the two horses which drew the van to stop. "Comrades, comrades!" they shouted. "Don't take your own brother to his death!" But the stupid brutes, too ignorant to realise what was happening, merely set back their ears and quickened their pace. Boxer's face did not reappear at the window. Too late, someone thought of racing ahead and shutting the five-barred gate; but in another moment the van was through it and rapidly disappearing down the road. Boxer was never seen again.

Three days later it was announced that he had died in the hospital at Willingdon, in spite of receiving every attention a horse could have. Squealer came to announce the news to the others. He had, he said, been present during Boxer's last hours.

"It was the most affecting sight I have ever seen!" said

Squealer, lifting his trotter and wiping away a tear. "I was at his bedside at the very last. And at the end, almost too weak to speak, he whispered in my ear that his sole sorrow was to have passed on before the windmill was finished. 'Forward, comrades!' he whispered. 'Forward in the name of the Rebellion. Long live Animal Farm! Long live Comrade Napoleon! Napoleon is always right.' Those were his very last words, comrades."

Here Squealer's demeanour suddenly changed. He fell silent for a moment, and his little eyes darted suspicious glances from side to side before he proceeded.

It had come to his knowledge, he said, that a foolish and wicked rumour had been circulated at the time of Boxer's removal. Some of the animals had noticed that the van which took Boxer away was marked "Horse Slaughterer", and had actually jumped to the conclusion that Boxer was being sent to the knacker's. It was almost unbelievable, said Squealer, that any animal could be so stupid. Surely, he cried indignantly, whisking his tail and skipping from side to side, surely they knew their beloved Leader, Comrade Napoleon, better than that? But the explanation was really very simple. The van had previously been the property of the knacker, and had been bought by the veterinary surgeon, who had not yet painted the old name out. That was how the mistake had arisen.

The animals were enormously relieved to hear this. And when Squealer went on to give further graphic details of Boxer's death-bed, the admirable care he had received, and the expensive medicines for which Napoleon had paid without a thought as to the cost, their last doubts disappeared and the sorrow that they felt for their comrade's death was tempered by the thought that at least he had died happy.

Napoleon himself appeared at the meeting on the following Sunday morning and pronounced a short oration in Boxer's honour. It had not been possible, he said, to bring back their lamented comrade's remains for interment on the farm, but he had ordered a large wreath to be made from the laurels in the farmhouse garden and sent down to be placed on Boxer's grave. And in a few days' time the pigs intended to hold a memorial banquet in Boxer's honour. Napoleon ended his speech with a reminder of Boxer's two favourite maxims, "I will work harder" and "Comrade Napoleon is always right"—maxims, he said, which every animal would do well to adopt as his own.

On the day appointed for the banquet, a grocer's van drove up from Willingdon and delivered a large wooden crate at the farmhouse. That night there was the sound of uproarious singing, which was followed by what sounded like a violent quarrel and ended at about eleven o'clock with a tremendous crash of glass. No one stirred in the farmhouse before noon on the following day, and the word went round that from somewhere or other the pigs had acquired the money to buy themselves another case of whisky.

CHAPTER 10

Years passed. The seasons came and went, the short animal lives fled by. A time came when there was no one who remembered the old days before the Rebellion, except Clover, Benjamin, Moses the raven, and a number of the pigs.

Muriel was dead; Bluebell, Jessie, and Pincher were dead. Jones too was dead—he had died in an inebriates' home in another part of the country. Snowball was forgotten. Boxer was forgotten, except by the few who had known him. Clover was an old stout mare now, stiff in the joints and with a tendency to rheumy eyes. She was two years past the retiring age, but in fact no animal had ever actually retired. The talk of setting aside a corner of the pasture for superannuated animals had long since been dropped. Napoleon was now a mature boar of twenty-four stone. Squealer was so fat that he could with difficulty see out of his eyes. Only old Benjamin was much the same as ever, except for being a little greyer about the muzzle, and, since Boxer's death, more morose and taciturn than ever.

There were many more creatures on the farm now, though the increase was not so great as had been expected in earlier years. Many animals had been born to whom the Rebellion was only a dim tradition, passed on by word of mouth, and others had been bought who had never heard mention of such a thing before their arrival. The farm possessed three horses now besides Clover. They were fine upstanding beasts, willing workers and good comrades, but very stupid. None of them proved able to learn the alphabet beyond the letter B. They accepted everything that they were told about the Rebellion and the principles of Animalism, especially from Clover, for whom they had an almost filial respect; but it was doubtful whether they understood very much of it.

The farm was more prosperous now, and better organised: it had even been enlarged by two fields which had been bought from Mr. Pilkington. The windmill had been successfully completed at last, and the farm possessed a threshing machine and a hay elevator of its own, and various new buildings had been added to it. Whymper had bought himself a dogcart. The windmill, however, had not after all been used for generating electrical power. It was used for milling corn, and brought in a handsome money profit. The animals were hard at work building yet another windmill; when that one was finished, so it was said, the dynamos would be installed. But the luxuries of which Snowball had once taught the animals to dream, the stalls with electric light and hot and cold water, and the three-day week, were no longer talked about. Napoleon had denounced such ideas as contrary to the spirit of Animalism. The truest happiness, he said, lay in working hard and living frugally.

Somehow it seemed as though the farm had grown richer without making the animals themselves any richer—except, of course, for the pigs and the dogs. Perhaps this was partly because there were so many pigs and so many dogs. It was not that these creatures did not work, after their fashion. There was, as Squealer was never tired of explaining, endless work in the supervision and organisation of the farm. Much of this work was of a kind that the other animals were too ignorant to understand. For example, Squealer told them that the pigs had to expend enormous labours every day upon mysterious things called "files", "reports", "minutes", and "memoranda". These were large sheets of paper which had to be closely covered with writing, and as soon as they were so covered, they were burnt in the furnace. This was of the highest importance for the welfare of the farm, Squealer said. But still, neither pigs nor dogs produced any food by their own labour; and there were very many of them, and their appetites were always good.

As for the others, their life, so far as they knew, was as it had always been. They were generally hungry, they slept on straw, they drank from the pool, they laboured in the fields; in winter they were troubled by the cold, and in summer by the flies. Sometimes the older ones among them racked their dim memories and tried to determine whether in the early days of the Rebellion, when Jones's expulsion was still recent, things had been better or worse than now. They could not remember. There was nothing with which they could compare their present lives: they had nothing to go upon except Squealer's lists of figures, which invariably demonstrated that everything was getting better and better. The animals found the problem insoluble; in any case, they had little time for speculating on such things now. Only old Benjamin professed to remember every detail of his long life and to know that things never had been, nor ever could be much better or much worse—hunger, hardship, and disappointment being, so he said, the unalterable law of life.

And yet the animals never gave up hope. More, they never lost, even for an instant, their sense of honour and privilege in being members of Animal Farm. They were still the only farm in the whole county—in all England!—owned and operated by animals. Not one of them, not even the youngest, not even the newcomers who had been brought from farms ten or twenty miles away, ever ceased to marvel at that. And when they heard the gun booming and saw the green flag fluttering at the masthead, their hearts swelled with imperishable pride, and the talk turned always towards the old heroic days, the expulsion of Jones, the writing of the Seven Commandments, the great battles in which the human invaders had been defeated. None of the old dreams had been abandoned. The Republic of the Animals which Major had foretold, when the green fields of England should be untrodden by human feet, was still believed in. Some day it was coming: it might not be soon, it might not be within the lifetime of any animal now living, but still it was coming. Even the tune of "Beasts of England" was perhaps hummed secretly here and there: at any rate, it was a fact that every animal on the farm knew it, though no one would have dared to sing it aloud. It might be that their lives were hard and that not all of their hopes had been fulfilled; but they were conscious that they were not as other animals. If they went hungry, it was not from feeding tyrannical human beings; if they worked hard, at least they worked for themselves. No creature among them went upon two legs. No creature called any other creature "Master". All animals were equal.

One day in early summer Squealer ordered the sheep to follow him, and led them out to a piece of waste ground at the other end of the farm, which had become overgrown with birch saplings. The sheep spent the whole day there browsing at the leaves under Squealer's supervision. In the evening he returned to the farmhouse himself, but, as it was warm weather, told the sheep to stay where they were. It ended by their remaining there for a whole week, during which time the other animals saw nothing of them. Squealer was with them for the greater part of every day. He was, he said, teaching them to sing a new song, for which privacy was needed.

It was just after the sheep had returned, on a pleasant

evening when the animals had finished work and were making their way back to the farm buildings, that the terrified neighing of a horse sounded from the yard. Startled, the animals stopped in their tracks. It was Clover's voice. She neighed again, and all the animals broke into a gallop and rushed into the yard. Then they saw what Clover had seen.

It was a pig walking on his hind legs.

Yes, it was Squealer. A little awkwardly, as though not quite used to supporting his considerable bulk in that position, but with perfect balance, he was strolling across the yard. And a moment later, out from the door of the farmhouse came a long file of pigs, all walking on their hind legs. Some did it better than others, one or two were even a trifle unsteady and looked as though they would have liked the support of a stick, but every one of them made his way right round the yard successfully. And finally there was a tremendous baying of dogs and a shrill crowing from the black cockerel, and out came Napoleon himself, majestically upright, casting haughty glances from side to side, and with his dogs gambolling round him.

He carried a whip in his trotter.

There was a deadly silence. Amazed, terrified, huddling together, the animals watched the long line of pigs march slowly round the yard. It was as though the world had turned upside-down. Then there came a moment when the first shock had worn off and when, in spite of everything—in spite of their terror of the dogs, and of the habit, developed through long years, of never complaining, never criticising, no matter what happened—they might have uttered some word of protest. But just at that moment, as though at a signal, all the sheep burst out into a tremendous bleating of—

"Four legs good, two legs *better*! Four legs good, two legs *better*! Four legs good, two legs *better*!"

It went on for five minutes without stopping. And by the time the sheep had quieted down, the chance to utter any protest had passed, for the pigs had marched back into the farmhouse.

Benjamin felt a nose nuzzling at his shoulder. He looked round. It was Clover. Her old eyes looked dimmer than ever. Without saying anything, she tugged gently at his mane and led him round to the end of the big barn, where the Seven Commandments were written. For a minute or two they stood gazing at the tatted wall with its white lettering.

"My sight is failing," she said finally. "Even when I was young I could not have read what was written there. But it appears to me that that wall looks different. Are the Seven Commandments the same as they used to be, Benjamin?"

For once Benjamin consented to break his rule, and he read out to her what was written on the wall. There was nothing there now except a single Commandment. It ran:

ALL ANIMALS ARE EQUAL BUT SOME ANIMALS
ARE MORE EQUAL THAN OTHERS.

After that it did not seem strange when next day the pigs who were supervising the work of the farm all carried whips in their trotters. It did not seem strange to learn that the pigs had bought themselves a wireless set, were arranging to install a telephone, and had taken out subscriptions to *John Bull*, *Tit-Bits*, and the *Daily Mirror*. It did not seem strange when Napoleon was seen strolling in the farmhouse garden with a pipe in his mouth—no, not even when the pigs took Mr. Jones's clothes out of the wardrobes and put them on, Napoleon himself appearing in a black coat, ratcatcher breeches, and leather leggings, while his favourite sow appeared in the watered silk dress which Mrs. Jones had been used to wear on Sundays.

A week later, in the afternoon, a number of dogcarts drove up to the farm. A deputation of neighbouring farmers had been invited to make a tour of inspection. They were shown all over the farm, and expressed great admiration for everything they saw, especially the windmill. The animals were weeding the turnip field. They worked diligently hardly raising their faces from the ground, and not knowing whether to be more frightened of the pigs or of the human visitors.

That evening loud laughter and bursts of singing came from the farmhouse. And suddenly, at the sound of the mingled voices, the animals were stricken with curiosity. What could be happening in there, now that for the first time animals and human beings were meeting on terms of equality? With one accord they began to creep as quietly as possible into the farmhouse garden.

At the gate they paused, half frightened to go on but Clover led the way in. They tiptoed up to the house, and such animals as were tall enough peered in at the dining-room window. There, round the long table, sat half a dozen farmers and half a dozen of the more eminent pigs, Napoleon himself occupying the seat of honour at the head of the table. The pigs appeared completely at ease in their chairs. The company had been enjoying a game of cards but had broken off for the moment, evidently in order to drink a toast. A large jug was circulating, and the mugs were being refilled with beer. No one noticed the wondering faces of the animals that gazed in at the window.

Mr. Pilkington, of Foxwood, had stood up, his mug in his hand. In a moment, he said, he would ask the present company to drink a toast. But before doing so, there were a few words that he felt it incumbent upon him to say.

It was a source of great satisfaction to him, he said—and, he was sure, to all others present—to feel that a long period of mistrust and misunderstanding had now come to an end. There had been a time—not that he, or any of the present company, had shared such sentiments—but there had been a time when the respected proprietors of Animal Farm had been regarded, he would not say with hostility, but perhaps with a certain measure of misgiving, by their human neighbours. Unfortunate incidents had occurred, mistaken ideas had been current. It had been felt that the existence of a farm owned and operated by pigs was somehow abnormal and was liable to have an unsettling effect in the neighbourhood. Too many farmers had assumed, without due enquiry, that on such a farm a spirit of licence and indiscipline would prevail. They had been nervous about the effects upon their own animals, or even upon their human employees. But all such doubts were now dispelled. Today he and his friends had visited Animal Farm and inspected every inch of it with their own eyes, and what did they find? Not only the most up-to-date methods, but a discipline and an orderliness which should be an example to all farmers everywhere. He believed that he was right in saying that the lower animals on Animal Farm did more work and received less food than any animals in the county. Indeed, he and his fellow-visitors today had observed many features which they intended to introduce on their own farms immediately.

He would end his remarks, he said, by emphasising once again the friendly feelings that subsisted, and ought to subsist, between Animal Farm and its neighbours. Between pigs and human beings there was not, and there need not be, any clash of interests whatever. Their struggles and their difficulties were one. Was not the labour problem the same everywhere? Here it became apparent that Mr. Pilkington was about to spring some carefully prepared witticism on the company, but for a moment he was too overcome by amusement to be able to utter it. After much choking, during which his various chins turned purple, he managed to get it out: "If you have your lower animals to contend with," he said, "we have our lower classes!" This *bon mot* set the table in a roar; and Mr. Pilkington once again congratulated the pigs on the low rations, the long working hours, and the general absence of pampering which he had observed on Animal Farm.

And now, he said finally, he would ask the company to rise to their feet and make certain that their glasses were full. "Gentlemen," concluded Mr. Pilkington, "gentlemen, I give you a toast: To the prosperity of Animal Farm!"

There was enthusiastic cheering and stamping of feet. Napoleon was so gratified that he left his place and came round the table to clink his mug against Mr. Pilkington's before emptying it. When the cheering had died down, Napoleon, who had remained on his feet, intimated that he too had a few words to say.

Like all of Napoleon's speeches, it was short and to the point. He too, he said, was happy that the period of misunderstanding was at an end. For a long time there had been rumours—circulated, he had reason to think, by some malignant enemy—that there was something subversive and even revolutionary in the outlook of himself and his colleagues. They had been credited with attempting to stir up rebellion among the animals on neighbouring farms. Nothing could be further from the truth! Their sole wish, now and in the past, was to live at peace and in normal business relations with their neighbours. This farm which he had the honour to control, he added, was a co-operative enterprise. The title-deeds, which were in his own possession, were owned by the pigs jointly.

He did not believe, he said, that any of the old suspicions still lingered, but certain changes had been made recently in the routine of the farm which should have the effect of promoting confidence still further. Hitherto the animals on the farm had had a rather foolish custom of addressing one another as "Comrade". This was to be suppressed. There had also been a very strange custom, whose origin was unknown, of marching every Sunday morning past a boar's skull which was nailed to a post in the garden. This, too, would be suppressed, and the skull had already been buried. His visitors might have observed, too, the green flag which flew from the masthead. If so, they would perhaps have noted that the white hoof and horn with which it had previously been marked had now been removed. It would be a plain green flag from now onwards.

He had only one criticism, he said, to make of Mr. Pilkington's excellent and neighbourly speech. Mr. Pilkington had referred throughout to "Animal Farm". He could not of course know—for he, Napoleon, was only now for the first time announcing it—that the name "Animal Farm" had been abolished. Henceforward the farm was to be known as "The Manor Farm"—which, he believed, was its correct and original name.

"Gentlemen," concluded Napoleon, "I will give you the same toast as before, but in a different form. Fill your glasses to the brim. Gentlemen, here is my toast: To the prosperity of the Manor Farm!"

There was the same hearty cheering as before, and the mugs were emptied to the dregs. But as the animals outside gazed at the scene, it seemed to them that some strange thing was happening. What was it that had altered in the faces of the pigs? Clover's old dim eyes flitted from one face to another. Some of them had five chins, some had four, some had three. But what was it that seemed to be melting and changing? Then, the applause having come to an end, the company took up their cards and continued the game that had been interrupted, and the animals crept silently away.

But they had not gone twenty yards when they stopped short. An uproar of voices was coming from the farmhouse. They rushed back and looked through the window again. Yes, a violent quarrel was in progress. There were shoutings, bangings on the table, sharp suspicious glances, furious denials. The source of the trouble appeared to be that Napoleon and Mr. Pilkington had each played an ace of spades simultaneously.

Twelve voices were shouting in anger, and they were all

alike. No question, now, what had happened to the faces of the pigs. The creatures outside looked from pig to man, and from man to pig, and from pig to man again; but already it was impossible to say which was which.

CLASSIC LITERATURE: WORDS AND PHRASES
adapted from the Collins English Dictionary

Accoucheur NOUN a male midwife or doctor ❑ *I think my sister must have had some general idea that I was a young offender whom an Accoucheur Policemen had taken up (on my birthday) and delivered over to her* (Great Expectations by Charles Dickens)

addled ADJ confused and unable to think properly ❑ *But she counted and counted till she got that addled* (The Adventures of Huckleberry Finn by Mark Twain)

admiration NOUN amazement or wonder ❑ *lifting up his hands and eyes by way of admiration* (Gulliver's Travels by Jonathan Swift)

afeard ADJ afeard means afraid ❑ *shake it—and don't be afeard* (The Adventures of Huckleberry Finn by Mark Twain)

affected VERB affected means to assume the appearance of ❑ *Hadst thou affected sweet divinity* (Doctor Faustus 5.2 by Christopher Marlowe)

aground ADV when a boat runs aground, it touches the ground in a shallow part of the water and gets stuck ❑ *what kep' you?—boat get aground?* (The Adventures of Huckleberry Finn by Mark Twain)

ague NOUN a fever in which the patient has alternate hot and cold shivering fits ❑ *his exposure to the wet and cold had brought on fever and ague* (Oliver Twist by Charles Dickens)

alchemy ADJ false or worthless ❑ *all wealth alchemy* (The Sun Rising by John Donne)

all alike PHRASE the same all the time ❑ *Love, all alike* (The Sun Rising by John Donne)

alow and aloft PHRASE alow means in the lower part or bottom, and aloft means on the top, so alow and aloft means on the top and in the bottom or throughout ❑ *Someone's turned the chest out alow and aloft* (Treasure Island by Robert Louis Stevenson)

ambuscade NOUN ambuscade is not a proper word. Tom means an ambush, which is when a group of people attack their enemies, after hiding and waiting for them ❑ *and so we would lie in ambuscade, as he called it* (The Adventures of Huckleberry Finn by Mark Twain)

amiable ADJ likeable or pleasant ❑ *Such amiable qualities must speak for themselves* (Pride and Prejudice by Jane Austen)

amulet NOUN an amulet is a charm thought to drive away evil spirits. ❑ *uttered phrases at once occult and familiar, like the amulet worn on the heart* (Silas Marner by George Eliot)

amusement NOUN here amusement means a strange and disturbing puzzle ❑ *this was an amusement the other way* (Robinson Crusoe by Daniel Defoe)

ancient NOUN an ancient was the flag displayed on a ship to show which country it belongs to. It is also called the ensign ❑ *her ancient and pendants out* (Robinson Crusoe by Daniel Defoe)

antic ADJ here antic means horrible or grotesque ❑ *armed and dressed after a very antic manner* (Gulliver's Travels by Jonathan Swift)

antics NOUN antics is an old word meaning clowns, or people who do silly things to make other people laugh ❑ *And point like antics at his triple crown* (Doctor Faustus 3.2 by Christopher Marlowe)

appanage NOUN an appanage is a living allowance ❏ *As if loveliness were not the special prerogative of woman–her legitimate appanage and heritage!* (*Jane Eyre* by Charlotte Brontë)

appended VERB appended means attached or added to ❏ *and these words appended* (*Treasure Island* by Robert Louis Stevenson)

approver NOUN an approver is someone who gives evidence against someone he used to work with ❏ *Mr. Noah Claypole: receiving a free pardon from the Crown in consequence of being admitted approver against Fagin* (*Oliver Twist* by Charles Dickens)

areas NOUN the areas is the space, below street level, in front of the basement of a house ❏ *The Dodger had a vicious propensity, too, of pulling the caps from the heads of small boys and tossing them down areas* (*Oliver Twist* by Charles Dickens)

argument NOUN theme or important idea or subject which runs through a piece of writing ❏ *Thrice needful to the argument which now* (*The Prelude* by William Wordsworth)

artificially ADV artfully or cleverly ❏ *and he with a sharp flint sharpened very artificially* (*Gulliver's Travels* by Jonathan Swift)

artist NOUN here artist means a skilled workman ❏ *This man was a most ingenious artist* (*Gulliver's Travels* by Jonathan Swift)

assizes NOUN assizes were regular court sessions which a visiting judge was in charge of ❏ *you shall hang at the next assizes* (*Treasure Island* by Robert Louis Stevenson)

attraction NOUN gravitation, or Newton's theory of gravitation ❏ *he predicted the same fate to attraction* (*Gulliver's Travels* by Jonathan Swift)

aver VERB to aver is to claim something strongly ❏ *for Jem Rodney, the mole catcher, averred that one evening as he was returning homeward* (*Silas Marner* by George Eliot)

baby NOUN here baby means doll, which is a child's toy that looks like a small person ❏ *and skilful dressing her baby* (*Gulliver's Travels* by Jonathan Swift)

bagatelle NOUN bagatelle is a game rather like billiards and pool ❏ *Breakfast had been ordered at a pleasant little tavern, a mile or so away upon the rising ground beyond the green; and there was a bagatelle board in the room, in case we should desire to unbend our minds after the solemnity.* (*Great Expectations* by Charles Dickens)

bah EXCLAM Bah is an exclamation of frustration or anger ❏ *"Bah," said Scrooge.* (*A Christmas Carol* by Charles Dickens)

bairn NOUN a northern word for child ❏ *Who has taught you those fine words, my bairn?* (*Wuthering Heights* by Emily Brontë)

bait VERB to bait means to stop on a journey to take refreshment ❏ *So, when they stopped to bait the horse, and ate and drank and enjoyed themselves, I could touch nothing that they touched, but kept my fast unbroken.* (*David Copperfield* by Charles Dickens)

balustrade NOUN a balustrade is a row of vertical columns that form railings ❏ *but I mean to say you might have got a hearse up that staircase, and taken it broadwise, with the splinter-bar towards the wall, and the door towards the balustrades: and done it easy* (*A Christmas Carol* by Charles Dickens)

bandbox NOUN a large lightweight box for carrying bonnets or hats ❏ *I am glad I bought my bonnet, if it is only for the fun of having another bandbox* (*Pride and Prejudice* by Jane Austen)

barren NOUN a barren here is a stretch or expanse of barren land ❏ *a line of upright stones, continued the* *length of the barren* (*Wuthering Heights* by Emily Brontë)

basin NOUN a basin was a cup without a handle ❏ *who is drinking his tea out of a basin* (*Wuthering Heights* by Emily Brontë)

battalia NOUN the order of battle ❏ *till I saw part of his army in battalia* (*Gulliver's Travels* by Jonathan Swift)

battery NOUN a Battery is a fort or a place where guns are positioned ❏ *You bring the lot to me, at that old Battery over yonder* (*Great Expectations* by Charles Dickens)

battledore and shuttlecock NOUN The game battledore and shuttlecock was an early version of the game now known as badminton. The aim of the early game was simply to keep the shuttlecock from hitting the ground. ❏ *Battledore and shuttlecock's a wery good game when you an't the shuttlecock and two lawyers the battledores, in which case it gets too excitin' to be pleasant* (*Pickwick Papers* by Charles Dickens)

beadle NOUN a beadle was a local official who had power over the poor ❏ *But these impertinences were speedily checked by the evidence of the surgeon, and the testimony of the beadle* (*Oliver Twist* by Charles Dickens)

bearings NOUN the bearings of a place are the measurements or directions that are used to find or locate it ❏ *the bearings of the island* (*Treasure Island* by Robert Louis Stevenson)

beaufet NOUN a beaufet was a sideboard ❏ *and sweet-cake from the beaufet* (*Emma* by Jane Austen)

beck NOUN a beck is a small stream ❏ *a beck which follows the bend of the glen* (*Wuthering Heights* by Emily Brontë)

bedight VERB decorated ❏ *and bedight with Christmas holly stuck into the top.* (*A Christmas Carol* by Charles Dickens)

Bedlam NOUN Bedlam was a lunatic asylum in London which had statues carved by Caius Gabriel Cibber at its entrance ❏ *Bedlam, and those carved maniacs at the gates* (*The Prelude* by William Wordsworth)

beeves NOUN oxen or castrated bulls which are animals used for pulling vehicles or carrying things ❏ *to deliver in every morning six beeves* (*Gulliver's Travels* by Jonathan Swift)

begot VERB created or caused ❏ *Begot in thee* (*On His Mistress* by John Donne)

behoof NOUN behoof means benefit ❏ *"Yes, young man," said he, releasing the handle of the article in question, retiring a step or two from my table, and speaking for the behoof of the landlord and waiter at the door* (*Great Expectations* by Charles Dickens)

berth NOUN a berth is a bed on a boat ❏ *this is the berth for me* (*Treasure Island* by Robert Louis Stevenson)

bevers NOUN a bever was a snack, or small portion of food, eaten between main meals ❏ *that buys me thirty meals a day and ten bevers* (*Doctor Faustus 2.1* by Christopher Marlowe)

bilge water NOUN the bilge is the widest part of a ship's bottom, and the bilge water is the dirty water that collects there ❏ *no gush of bilge-water had turned it to fetid puddle* (*Jane Eyre* by Charlotte Brontë)

bills NOUN bills is an old term meaning prescription. A prescription is the piece of paper on which your doctor writes an order for medicine and which you give to a chemist to get the medicine ❏ *Are not thy bills hung up as monuments* (*Doctor Faustus 1.1* by Christopher Marlowe)

black cap NOUN a judge wore a black cap when he was about to sentence a prisoner to death ❑ *The judge assumed the black cap, and the prisoner still stood with the same air and gesture.* (*Oliver Twist* by Charles Dickens)

boot-jack NOUN a wooden device to help take boots off ❑ *The speaker appeared to throw a boot-jack, or some such article, at the person he addressed* (*Oliver Twist* by Charles Dickens)

booty NOUN booty means treasure or prizes ❑ *would be inclined to give up their booty in payment of the dead man's debts* (*Treasure Island* by Robert Louis Stevenson)

Bow Street runner PHRASE Bow Street runners were the first British police force, set up by the author Henry Fielding in the eighteenth century ❑ *as would have convinced a judge or a Bow Street runner* (*Treasure Island* by Robert Louis Stevenson)

brawn NOUN brawn is a dish of meat which is set in jelly ❑ *Heaped up upon the floor, to form a kind of throne, were turkeys, geese, game, poultry, brawn, great joints of meat, suckling-pigs* (*A Christmas Carol* by Charles Dickens)

bray VERB when a donkey brays, it makes a loud, harsh sound ❑ *and she doesn't bray like a jackass* (*The Adventures of Huckleberry Finn* by Mark Twain)

break VERB in order to train a horse you first have to break it ❑ *"If a high-mettled creature like this," said he, "can't be broken by fair means, she will never be good for anything"* (*Black Beauty* by Anna Sewell)

bullyragging VERB bullyragging is an old word which means bullying. To bullyrag someone is to threaten or force someone to do something they don't want to do ❑ *and a lot of loafers bullyragging him for sport* (*The Adventures of Huckleberry Finn* by Mark Twain)

but PREP except for (this) ❑ *but this, all pleasures fancies be* (*The Good-Morrow* by John Donne)

by hand PHRASE by hand was a common expression of the time meaning that baby had been fed either using a spoon or a bottle rather than by breast-feeding ❑ *My sister, Mrs. Joe Gargery, was more than twenty years older than I, and had established a great reputation with herself . . . because she had bought me up "by hand"* (*Great Expectations* by Charles Dickens)

bye-spots NOUN bye-spots are lonely places ❑ *and bye-spots of tales rich with indigenous produce* (*The Prelude* by William Wordsworth)

calico NOUN calico is plain white fabric made from cotton ❑ *There was two old dirty calico dresses* (*The Adventures of Huckleberry Finn* by Mark Twain)

camp-fever NOUN camp-fever was another word for the disease typhus ❑ *during a severe camp-fever* (*Emma* by Jane Austen)

cant NOUN cant is insincere or empty talk ❑ *"Man," said the Ghost, "if man you be in heart, not adamant, forbear that wicked cant until you have discovered What the surplus is, and Where it is."* (*A Christmas Carol* by Charles Dickens)

canty ADJ canty means lively, full of life ❑ *My mother lived til eighty, a canty dame to the last* (*Wuthering Heights* by Emily Brontë)

canvas VERB to canvas is to discuss ❑ *We think so very differently on this point Mr Knightley, that there can be no use in canvassing it* (*Emma* by Jane Austen)

capital ADJ capital means excellent or extremely good ❑ *for it's capital, so shady, light, and big* (*Little Women* by Louisa May Alcott)

capstan NOUN a capstan is a device used on a ship to lift sails and anchors ❑ *capstans going, ships going out to sea, and unintelligible sea creatures roaring curses over the* *bulwarks at respondent lightermen* (*Great Expectations* by Charles Dickens)

case-bottle NOUN a square bottle designed to fit with others into a case ❑ *The spirit being set before him in a huge case-bottle, which had originally come out of some ship's locker* (*The Old Curiosity Shop* by Charles Dickens)

casement NOUN casement is a word meaning window. The teacher in *Nicholas Nickleby* misspells window showing what a bad teacher he is ❑ *W-i-n, win, d-e-r, der, winder, a casement.* (*Nicholas Nickleby* by Charles Dickens)

cataleptic ADJ a cataleptic fit is one in which the victim goes into a trancelike state and remains still for a long time ❑ *It was at this point in their history that Silas's cataleptic fit occurred during the prayer-meeting* (*Silas Marner* by George Eliot)

cauldron NOUN a cauldron is a large cooking pot made of metal ❑ *stirring a large cauldron which seemed to be full of soup* (*Alice's Adventures in Wonderland* by Lewis Carroll)

cephalic ADJ cephalic means to do with the head ❑ *with ink composed of a cephalic tincture* (*Gulliver's Travels* by Jonathan Swift)

chaise and four NOUN a closed four-wheel carriage pulled by four horses ❑ *he came down on Monday in a chaise and four to see the place* (*Pride and Prejudice* by Jane Austen)

chamberlain NOUN the main servant in a household ❑ *In those times a bed was always to be got there at any hour of the night, and the chamberlain, letting me in at his ready wicket, lighted the candle next in order on his shelf* (*Great Expectations* by Charles Dickens)

characters NOUN distinguishing marks ❑ *Impressed upon all forms the characters* (*The Prelude* by William Wordsworth)

chary ADJ cautious ❑ *I should have been chary of discussing my guardian too freely even with her* (*Great Expectations* by Charles Dickens)

cherishes VERB here cherishes means cheers or brightens ❑ *some philosophic song of Truth that cherishes our daily life* (*The Prelude* by William Wordsworth)

chickens' meat PHRASE chickens' meat is an old term which means chickens' feed or food ❑ *I had shook a bag of chickens' meat out in that place* (*Robinson Crusoe* by Daniel Defoe)

chimeras NOUN a chimera is an unrealistic idea or a wish which is unlikely to be fulfilled ❑ *with many other wild impossible chimeras* (*Gulliver's Travels* by Jonathan Swift)

chines NOUN chine is a cut of meat that includes part or all of the backbone of the animal ❑ *and they found hams and chines uncut* (*Silas Marner* by George Eliot)

chits NOUN chits is a slang word which means girls ❑ *I hate affected, niminy-piminy chits!* (*Little Women* by Louisa May Alcott)

chopped VERB chopped means come suddenly or accidentally ❑ *if I had chopped upon them* (*Robinson Crusoe* by Daniel Defoe)

chute NOUN a narrow channel ❑ *One morning about day-break, I found a canoe and crossed over a chute to the main shore* (*The Adventures of Huckleberry Finn* by Mark Twain)

circumspection NOUN careful observation of events and circumstances; caution ❑ *I honour your circumspection* (*Pride and Prejudice* by Jane Austen)

clambered VERB clambered means to climb somewhere with difficulty, usually using your hands and your feet ❑ *he clambered up and down stairs* (*Treasure Island* by Robert Louis Stevenson)

clime NOUN climate ❑ *no season knows nor clime* (*The Sun Rising* by John Donne)

clinched VERB clenched ❑ *the tops whereof I could but just reach with my fist clinched* (*Gulliver's Travels* by Jonathan Swift)

close chair NOUN a close chair is a sedan chair, which is an covered chair which has room for one person. The sedan chair is carried on two poles by two men, one in front and one behind ❑ *persuaded even the Empress herself to let me hold her in her close chair* (*Gulliver's Travels* by Jonathan Swift)

clown NOUN clown here means peasant or person who lives off the land ❑ *In ancient days by emperor and clown* (*Ode on a Nightingale* by John Keats)

coalheaver NOUN a coalheaver loaded coal onto ships using a spade ❑ *Good, strong, wholesome medicine, as was given with great success to two Irish labourers and a coalheaver* (*Oliver Twist* by Charles Dickens)

coal-whippers NOUN men who worked at docks using machines to load coal onto ships ❑ *here, were colliers by the score and score, with the coal-whippers plunging off stages on deck* (*Great Expectations* by Charles Dickens)

cobweb NOUN a cobweb is the net which a spider makes for catching insects ❑ *the walls and ceilings were all hung round with cobwebs* (*Gulliver's Travels* by Jonathan Swift)

coddling VERB coddling means to treat someone too kindly or protect them too much ❑ *and I've been coddling the fellow as if I'd been his grand-mother* (*Little Women* by Louisa May Alcott)

coil NOUN coil means noise or fuss or disturbance ❑ *What a coil is there?* (*Doctor Faustus 4.7* by Christopher Marlowe)

collared VERB to collar something is a slang term which means to capture.

In this sentence, it means he stole it [the money] ❑ *he collared it* (*The Adventures of Huckleberry Finn* by Mark Twain)

colling VERB colling is an old word which means to embrace and kiss ❑ *and no clasping and colling at all* (*Tess of the D'Urbervilles* by Thomas Hardy)

colloquies NOUN colloquy is a formal conversation or dialogue ❑ *Such colloquies have occupied many a pair of pale-faced weavers* (*Silas Marner* by George Eliot)

comfit NOUN sugar-covered pieces of fruit or nut eaten as sweets ❑ *and pulled out a box of comfits* (*Alice's Adventures in Wonderland* by Lewis Carroll)

coming out VERB when a girl came out in society it meant she was of marriageable age. In order to "come out" girls were expecting to attend balls and other parties during a season ❑ *The younger girls formed hopes of coming out a year or two sooner than they might otherwise have done* (*Pride and Prejudice* by Jane Austen)

commit VERB commit means arrest or stop ❑ *Commit the rascals* (*Doctor Faustus 4.7* by Christopher Marlowe)

commodious ADJ commodious means convenient ❑ *the most commodious and effectual ways* (*Gulliver's Travels* by Jonathan Swift)

commons NOUN commons is an old term meaning food shared with others ❑ *his pauper assistants ranged themselves behind him; the gruel was served out; and a long grace was said over the short commons.* (*Oliver Twist* by Charles Dickens)

complacency NOUN here complacency means a desire to please others. To-day complacency means feeling pleased with oneself without good reason. ❑ *Twas thy power that raised the first complacency in me* (*The Prelude* by William Wordsworth)

complaisance NOUN complaisance was eagerness to please ❑ *we cannot wonder at his complaisance* (*Pride and Prejudice* by Jane Austen)

complaisant ADJ complaisant means polite ❑ *extremely cheerful and complaisant to their guest* (*Gulliver's Travels* by Jonathan Swift)

conning VERB conning means learning by heart ❑ *Or conning more* (*The Prelude* by William Wordsworth)

consequent NOUN consequence ❑ *as avarice is the necessary consequent of old age* (*Gulliver's Travels* by Jonathan Swift)

consorts NOUN concerts ❑ *The King, who delighted in music, had frequent consorts at Court* (*Gulliver's Travels* by Jonathan Swift)

conversible ADJ conversible meant easy to talk to, companionable ❑ *He can be a conversible companion* (*Pride and Prejudice* by Jane Austen)

copper NOUN a copper is a large pot that can be heated directly over a fire ❑ *He gazed in stupefied astonishment on the small rebel for some seconds, and then clung for support to the copper* (*Oliver Twist* by Charles Dickens)

copper-stick NOUN a copper-stick is the long piece of wood used to stir washing in the copper (or boiler) which was usually the biggest cooking pot in the house ❑ *It was Christmas Eve, and I had to stir the pudding for next day, with a copper-stick, from seven to eight by the Dutch clock* (*Great Expectations* by Charles Dickens)

counting-house NOUN a counting-house is a place where accountants work ❑ *Once upon a time–of all the good days in the year, on Christmas Eve–old Scrooge sat busy in his counting-house* (*A Christmas Carol* by Charles Dickens)

courtier NOUN a courtier is someone who attends the king or queen–a member of the court ❑ *next the ten courtiers;* (*Alice's Adventures in Wonderland* by Lewis Carroll)

covies NOUN covies were flocks of partridges ❑ *and will save all of the best covies for you* (*Pride and Prejudice* by Jane Austen)

cowed VERB cowed means frightened or intimidated ❑ *it cowed me more than the pain* (*Treasure Island* by Robert Louis Stevenson)

cozened VERB cozened means tricked or deceived ❑ *Do you remember, sir, how you cozened me* (*Doctor Faustus 4.7* by Christopher Marlowe)

cravats NOUN a cravat is a folded cloth that a man wears wrapped around his neck as a decorative item of clothing ❑ *we'd 'a' slept in our cravats to-night* (*The Adventures of Huckleberry Finn* by Mark Twain)

crock and dirt PHRASE crock and dirt is an old expression meaning soot and dirt ❑ *and the mare catching cold at the door, and the boy grimed with crock and dirt* (*Great Expectations* by Charles Dickens)

crockery NOUN here crockery means pottery ❑ *By one of the parrots was a cat made of crockery* (*The Adventures of Huckleberry Finn* by Mark Twain)

crooked sixpence PHRASE it was considered unlucky to have a bent sixpence ❑ *You've got the beauty, you see, and I've got the luck, so you must keep me by you for your crooked sixpence* (*Silas Marner* by George Eliot)

croquet NOUN croquet is a traditional English summer game in which players try to hit wooden balls through hoops ❑ *and once she remembered trying to box her own ears for having cheated herself in a game of croquet* (*Alice's Adventures in Wonderland* by Lewis Carroll)

cross PREP across ❑ *The two great streets, which run cross and divide it into four quarters* (*Gulliver's Travels* by Jonathan Swift)

culpable ADJ if you are culpable for something it means you are to blame ❑ *deep are the sorrows that spring from false ideas for which no man is culpable.* (*Silas Marner* by George Eliot)

cultured ADJ cultivated ❑ *Nor less when spring had warmed the cultured Vale* (*The Prelude* by William Wordsworth)

cupidity NOUN cupidity is greed ❑ *These people hated me with the hatred of cupidity and disappointment.* (*Great Expectations* by Charles Dickens)

curricle NOUN an open two-wheeled carriage with one seat for the driver and space for a single passenger ❑ *and they saw a lady and a gentleman in a curricle* (*Pride and Prejudice* by Jane Austen)

cynosure NOUN a cynosure is something that strongly attracts attention or admiration ❑ *Then I thought of Eliza and Georgiana; I beheld one the cynosure of a ballroom, the other the inmate of a convent cell* (*Jane Eyre* by Charlotte Brontë)

dalliance NOUN someone's dalliance with something is a brief involvement with it ❑ *nor sporting in the dalliance of love* (*Doctor Faustus Chorus* by Christopher Marlowe)

darkling ADV darkling is an archaic way of saying in the dark ❑ *Darkling I listen* (*Ode on a Nightingale* by John Keats)

delf-case NOUN a sideboard for holding dishes and crockery ❑ *at the pewter dishes and delf-case* (*Wuthering Heights* by Emily Brontë)

determined ■ VERB here determined means ended ❑ *and be out of vogue when that was determined* (*Gulliver's Travels* by Jonathan Swift) ■ VERB determined can mean to have been learned or found especially by investigation or experience ❑ *All the sensitive feelings it wounded so cruelly, all the shame and misery it kept alive within my breast, became more poignant as I*

thought of this; and I determined that the life was unendurable (*David Copperfield* by Charles Dickens)

Deuce NOUN a slang term for the Devil ❑ *Ah, I dare say I did. Deuce take me, he added suddenly, I know I did. I find I am not quite unscrewed yet.* (*Great Expectations* by Charles Dickens)

diabolical ADJ diabolical means devilish or evil ❑ *and with a thousand diabolical expressions* (*Treasure Island* by Robert Louis Stevenson)

direction NOUN here direction means address ❑ *Elizabeth was not surprised at it, as Jane had written the direction remarkably ill* (*Pride and Prejudice* by Jane Austen)

discover VERB to make known or announce ❑ *the Emperor would discover the secret while I was out of his power* (*Gulliver's Travels* by Jonathan Swift)

dissemble VERB hide or conceal ❑ *Dissemble nothing* (*On His Mistress* by John Donne)

dissolve VERB dissolve here means to release from life, to die ❑ *Fade far away, dissolve, and quite forget* (*Ode on a Nightingale* by John Keats)

distrain VERB to distrain is to seize the property of someone who is in debt in compensation for the money owed ❑ *for he's threatening to distrain for it* (*Silas Marner* by George Eliot)

Divan NOUN a Divan was originally a Turkish council of state–the name was transferred to the couches they sat on and is used to mean this in English ❑ *Mr Brass applauded this picture very much, and the bed being soft and comfortable, Mr Quilp determined to use it, both as a sleeping place by night and as a kind of Divan by day.* (*The Old Curiosity Shop* by Charles Dickens)

divorcement NOUN separation ❑ *By all pains which want and divorcement* *hath* (*On His Mistress* by John Donne)

dog in the manger, PHRASE this phrase describes someone who prevents you from enjoying something that they themselves have no need for ❏ *You are a dog in the manger, Cathy, and desire no one to be loved but yourself* (*Wuthering Heights* by Emily Brontë)

dolorifuge NOUN dolorifuge is a word which Thomas Hardy invented. It means pain-killer or comfort ❏ *as a species of dolorifuge* (*Tess of the D'Urbervilles* by Thomas Hardy)

dome NOUN building ❏ *that river and that mouldering dome* (*The Prelude* by William Wordsworth)

domestic NOUN here domestic means a person's management of the house ❏ *to give some account of my domestic* (*Gulliver's Travels* by Jonathan Swift)

dunce NOUN a dunce is another word for idiot ❏ *Do you take me for a dunce? Go on?* (*Alice's Adventures in Wonderland* by Lewis Carroll)

Ecod EXCLAM a slang exclamation meaning "oh God!" ❏ *"Ecod," replied Wemmick, shaking his head, "that's not my trade."* (*Great Expectations* by Charles Dickens)

egg-hot NOUN an egg-hot (see also "flip" and "negus") was a hot drink made from beer and eggs, sweetened with nutmeg ❏ *She fainted when she saw me return, and made a little jug of egg-hot afterwards to console us while we talked it over.* (*David Copperfield* by Charles Dickens)

encores NOUN an encore is a short extra performance at the end of a longer one, which the entertainer gives because the audience has enthusiastically asked for it ❏ *we want a little something to answer encores with, anyway* (*The Adventures of Huckleberry Finn* by Mark Twain)

equipage NOUN an elegant and impressive carriage ❏ *and besides, the equipage did not answer to any of*

their neighbours (*Pride and Prejudice* by Jane Austen)

exordium NOUN an exordium is the opening part of a speech ❏ *"Now, Handel," as if it were the grave beginning of a portentous business exordium, he had suddenly given up that tone* (*Great Expectations* by Charles Dickens)

expect VERB here expect means to wait for ❏ *to expect his farther commands* (*Gulliver's Travels* by Jonathan Swift)

familiars NOUN familiars means spirits or devils who come to someone when they are called ❏ *I'll turn all the lice about thee into familiars* (*Doctor Faustus 1.4* by Christopher Marlowe)

fantods NOUN a fantod is a person who fidgets or can't stop moving nervously ❏ *It most give me the fantods* (*The Adventures of Huckleberry Finn* by Mark Twain)

farthing NOUN a farthing is an old unit of British currency which was worth a quarter of a penny ❏ *Not a farthing less. A great many back-payments are included in it, I assure you.* (*A Christmas Carol* by Charles Dickens)

farthingale NOUN a hoop worn under a skirt to extend it ❏ *A bell with an old voice–which I dare say in its time had often said to the house, Here is the green farthingale* (*Great Expectations* by Charles Dickens)

favours NOUN here favours is an old word which means ribbons ❏ *A group of humble mourners entered the gate: wearing white favours* (*Oliver Twist* by Charles Dickens)

feigned VERB pretend or pretending ❏ *not my feigned page* (*On His Mistress* by John Donne)

fence ■ NOUN a fence is someone who receives and sells stolen goods ❏ *What are you up to? Ill-treating the boys, you covetous, avaricious, in-sa-ti-a-ble old fence?* (*Oliver Twist* by

Charles Dickens) ■ NOUN defence or protection ❑ *but honesty hath no fence against superior cunning* (*Gulliver's Travels* by Jonathan Swift)

fess VERB fess is an old word which means pleased or proud ❑ *You'll be fess enough, my poppet* (*Tess of the D'Urbervilles* by Thomas Hardy)

fettered ADJ fettered means bound in chains or chained ❑ *"You are fettered," said Scrooge, trembling. "Tell me why?"* (*A Christmas Carol* by Charles Dickens)

fidges VERB fidges means fidgets, which is to keep moving your hands slightly because you are nervous or excited ❑ *Look, Jim, how my fingers fidges* (*Treasure Island* by Robert Louis Stevenson)

finger-post NOUN a finger-post is a sign-post showing the direction to different places ❑ *"The gallows," continued Fagin, "the gallows, my dear, is an ugly finger-post, which points out a very short and sharp turning that has stopped many a bold fellow's career on the broad highway."* (*Oliver Twist* by Charles Dickens)

fire-irons NOUN fire-irons are tools kept by the side of the fire to either cook with or look after the fire ❑ *the fire-irons came first* (*Alice's Adventures in Wonderland* by Lewis Carroll)

fire-plug NOUN a fire-plug is another word for a fire hydrant ❑ *The pony looked with great attention into a fire-plug, which was near him, and appeared to be quite absorbed in contemplating it* (*The Old Curiosity Shop* by Charles Dickens)

flank NOUN flank is the side of an animal ❑ *And all her silken flanks with garlands dressed* (*Ode on a Grecian Urn* by John Keats)

flip NOUN a flip is a drink made from warmed ale, sugar, spice and beaten egg ❑ *The events of the day, in combination with the twins, if not with the flip, had made Mrs. Micawber hysterical, and she shed tears as she replied* (*David Copperfield* by Charles Dickens)

flit VERB flit means to move quickly ❑ *and if he had meant to flit to Thrushcross Grange* (*Wuthering Heights* by Emily Brontë)

floorcloth NOUN a floorcloth was a hard-wearing piece of canvas used instead of carpet ❑ *This avenging phantom was ordered to be on duty at eight on Tuesday morning in the hall (it was two feet square, as charged for floorcloth)* (*Great Expectations* by Charles Dickens)

fly-driver NOUN a fly-driver is a carriage drawn by a single horse ❑ *The fly-drivers, among whom I inquired next, were equally jocose and equally disrespectful* (*David Copperfield* by Charles Dickens)

fob NOUN a small pocket in which a watch is kept ❑ *"Certain," replied the man, drawing a gold watch from his fob* (*Oliver Twist* by Charles Dickens)

folly NOUN folly means foolishness or stupidity ❑ *the folly of beginning a work* (*Robinson Crusoe* by Daniel Defoe)

fond ADJ fond means foolish ❑ *Fond worldling* (*Doctor Faustus 5.2* by Christopher Marlowe)

fondness NOUN silly or foolish affection ❑ *They have no fondness for their colts or foals* (*Gulliver's Travels* by Jonathan Swift)

for his fancy PHRASE for his fancy means for his liking or as he wanted ❑ *and as I did not obey quick enough for his fancy* (*Treasure Island* by Robert Louis Stevenson)

forlorn ADJ lost or very upset ❑ *you are from that day forlorn* (*Gulliver's Travels* by Jonathan Swift)

foster-sister NOUN a foster-sister was someone brought up by the same nurse or in the same household ❑ *I had been his foster-sister* (*Wuthering Heights* by Emily Brontë)

fox-fire NOUN fox-fire is a weak glow that is given off by decaying, rotten wood ❑ *what we must have was a lot of them rotten chunks that's called fox-fire* (The Adventures of Huckleberry Finn by Mark Twain)

frozen sea PHRASE the Arctic Ocean ❑ *into the frozen sea* (Gulliver's Travels by Jonathan Swift)

gainsay VERB to gainsay something is to say it isn't true or to deny it ❑ *"So she had," cried Scrooge. "You're right. I'll not gainsay it, Spirit. God forbid!"* (A Christmas Carol by Charles Dickens)

gaiters NOUN gaiters were leggings made of a cloth or piece of leather which covered the leg from the knee to the ankle ❑ *Mr Knightley was hard at work upon the lower buttons of his thick leather gaiters* (Emma by Jane Austen)

galluses NOUN galluses is an old spelling of gallows, and here means suspenders. Suspenders are straps worn over someone's shoulders and fastened to their trousers to prevent the trousers falling down ❑ *and home-knit galluses* (The Adventures of Huckleberry Finn by Mark Twain)

galoot NOUN a sailor but also a clumsy person ❑ *and maybe a galoot on it chopping* (The Adventures of Huckleberry Finn by Mark Twain)

gayest ADJ gayest means the most lively and bright or merry ❑ *Beth played her gayest march* (Little Women by Louisa May Alcott)

gem NOUN here gem means jewellery ❑ *the mountain shook off turf and flower, had only heath for raiment and crag for gem* (Jane Eyre by Charlotte Brontë)

giddy ADJ giddy means dizzy ❑ *and I wish you wouldn't keep appearing and vanishing so suddenly; you make one quite giddy.* (Alice's Adventures in Wonderland by Lewis Carroll)

gig NOUN a light two-wheeled carriage ❑ *when a gig drove up to the garden gate: out of which there jumped a fat gentleman* (Oliver Twist by Charles Dickens)

gladsome ADJ gladsome is an old word meaning glad or happy ❑ *Nobody ever stopped him in the street to say, with gladsome looks* (A Christmas Carol by Charles Dickens)

glen NOUN a glen is a small valley; the word is used commonly in Scotland ❑ *a beck which follows the bend of the glen* (Wuthering Heights by Emily Brontë)

gravelled VERB gravelled is an old term which means to baffle or defeat someone ❑ *Gravelled the pastors of the German Church* (Doctor Faustus 1.1 by Christopher Marlowe)

grinder NOUN a grinder was a private tutor ❑ *but that when he had had the happiness of marrying Mrs Pocket very early in his life, he had impaired his prospects and taken up the calling of a Grinder* (Great Expectations by Charles Dickens)

gruel NOUN gruel is a thin, watery cornmeal or oatmeal soup ❑ *and the little saucepan of gruel (Scrooge had a cold in his head) upon the hob.* (A Christmas Carol by Charles Dickens)

guinea, half a NOUN half a guinea was ten shillings and sixpence ❑ *but lay out half a guinea at Ford's* (Emma by Jane Austen)

gull VERB gull is an old term which means to fool or deceive someone ❑ *Hush, I'll gull him supernaturally* (Doctor Faustus 3.4 by Christopher Marlowe)

gunnel NOUN the gunnel, or gunwale, is the upper edge of a boat's side ❑ *But he put his foot on the gunnel and rocked her* (The Adventures of Huckleberry Finn by Mark Twain)

gunwale NOUN the side of a ship ❑ *He dipped his hand in the water over the boat's gunwale* (Great Expectations by Charles Dickens)

Gytrash NOUN a Gytrash is an omen of misfortune to the superstitious, usually taking the form of a hound ❑ *I remembered certain of Bessie's tales, wherein figured a North-of-England spirit, called a "Gytrash"* (*Jane Eyre* by Charlotte Brontë)

hackney-cabriolet NOUN a two-wheeled carriage with four seats for hire and pulled by a horse ❑ *A hackney-cabriolet was in waiting; with the same vehemence which she had exhibited in addressing Oliver, the girl pulled him in with her, and drew the curtains close.* (*Oliver Twist* by Charles Dickens)

hackney-coach NOUN a four-wheeled horse-drawn vehicle for hire ❑ *The twilight was beginning to close in, when Mr. Brownlow alighted from a hackney-coach at his own door, and knocked softly.* (*Oliver Twist* by Charles Dickens)

haggler NOUN a haggler is someone who travels from place to place selling small goods and items ❑ *when I be plain Jack Durbeyfield, the haggler* (*Tess of the D'Urbervilles* by Thomas Hardy)

halter NOUN a halter is a rope or strap used to lead an animal or to tie it up ❑ *I had of course long been used to a halter and a headstall* (*Black Beauty* by Anna Sewell)

hamlet NOUN a hamlet is a small village or a group of houses in the countryside ❑ *down from the hamlet* (*Treasure Island* by Robert Louis Stevenson)

hand-barrow NOUN a hand-barrow is a device for carrying heavy objects. It is like a wheelbarrow except that it has handles, rather than wheels, for moving the barrow ❑ *his sea chest following behind him in a hand-barrow* (*Treasure Island* by Robert Louis Stevenson)

handspike NOUN a handspike was a stick which was used as a lever ❑ *a bit of stick like a handspike* (*Treasure Island* by Robert Louis Stevenson)

haply ADV haply means by chance or perhaps ❑ *And haply the Queen-Moon is on her throne* (*Ode on a Nightingale* by John Keats)

harem NOUN the harem was the part of the house where the women lived ❑ *mostly they hang round the harem* (*The Adventures of Huckleberry Finn* by Mark Twain)

hautboys NOUN hautboys are oboes ❑ *sausages and puddings resembling flutes and hautboys* (*Gulliver's Travels* by Jonathan Swift)

hawker NOUN a hawker is someone who sells goods to people as he travels rather than from a fixed place like a shop ❑ *to buy some stockings from a hawker* (*Treasure Island* by Robert Louis Stevenson)

hawser NOUN a hawser is a rope used to tie up or tow a ship or boat ❑ *Again among the tiers of shipping, in and out, avoiding rusty chain-cables, frayed hempen hawsers* (*Great Expectations* by Charles Dickens)

headstall NOUN the headstall is the part of the bridle or halter that goes around a horse's head ❑ *I had of course long been used to a halter and a headstall* (*Black Beauty* by Anna Sewell)

hearken VERB hearken means to listen ❑ *though we sometimes stopped to lay hold of each other and hearken* (*Treasure Island* by Robert Louis Stevenson)

heartless ADJ here heartless means without heart or dejected ❑ *I am not heartless* (*The Prelude* by William Wordsworth)

hebdomadal ADJ hebdomadal means weekly ❑ *It was the hebdomadal treat to which we all looked forward from Sabbath to Sabbath* (*Jane Eyre* by Charlotte Brontë)

highwaymen NOUN highwaymen were people who stopped travellers and robbed them ❑ *We are high-waymen* (*The Adventures of Huckleberry Finn* by Mark Twain)

hinds NOUN hinds means farm hands, or people who work on a farm ❑ *He called his hinds about him* (*Gulliver's Travels* by Jonathan Swift)

histrionic ADJ if you refer to someone's behaviour as histrionic, you are being critical of it because it is dramatic and exaggerated ❑ *But the histrionic muse is the darling* (*The Adventures of Huckleberry Finn* by Mark Twain)

hogs NOUN hogs is another word for pigs ❑ *Tom called the hogs "ingots"* (*The Adventures of Huckleberry Finn* by Mark Twain)

horrors NOUN the horrors are a fit, called delirium tremens, which is caused by drinking too much alcohol ❑ *I'll have the horrors* (*Treasure Island* by Robert Louis Stevenson)

huffy ADJ huffy means to be obviously annoyed or offended about something ❑ *They will feel that more than angry speeches or huffy actions* (*Little Women* by Louisa May Alcott)

hulks NOUN hulks were prison-ships ❑ *The miserable companion of thieves and ruffians, the fallen outcast of low haunts, the associate of the scourings of the jails and hulks* (*Oliver Twist* by Charles Dickens)

humbug NOUN humbug means nonsense or rubbish ❑ *"Bah," said Scrooge. "Humbug!"* (*A Christmas Carol* by Charles Dickens)

humours NOUN it was believed that there were four fluids in the body called humours which decided the temperament of a person depending on how much of each fluid was present ❑ *other peccant humours* (*Gulliver's Travels* by Jonathan Swift)

husbandry NOUN husbandry is farming animals ❑ *bad husbandry were plentifully anointing their wheels* (*Silas Marner* by George Eliot)

huswife NOUN a huswife was a small sewing kit ❑ *but I had put my huswife on it* (*Emma* by Jane Austen)

ideal ADJ ideal in this context means imaginary ❑ *I discovered the yell was not ideal* (*Wuthering Heights* by Emily Brontë)

If our two PHRASE if both our ❑ *If our two loves be one* (*The Good-Morrow* by John Donne)

ignis-fatuus NOUN ignis-fatuus is the light given out by burning marsh gases, which lead careless travellers into danger ❑ *it is madness in all women to let a secret love kindle within them, which, if unreturned and unknown, must devour the life that feeds it; and, if discovered and responded to, must lead ignis-fatuus-like, into miry wilds whence there is no extrication.* (*Jane Eyre* by Charlotte Brontë)

imaginations NOUN here imaginations means schemes or plans ❑ *soon drove out those imaginations* (*Gulliver's Travels* by Jonathan Swift)

impressible ADJ impressible means open or impressionable ❑ *for Marner had one of those impressible, self-doubting natures* (*Silas Marner* by George Eliot)

in good intelligence PHRASE friendly with each other ❑ *that these two persons were in good intelligence with each other* (*Gulliver's Travels* by Jonathan Swift)

inanity NOUN inanity is silliness or dull stupidity ❑ *Do we not wile away moments of inanity* (*Silas Marner* by George Eliot)

incivility NOUN incivility means rudeness or impoliteness ❑ *if it's only for a piece of incivility like to-night's* (*Treasure Island* by Robert Louis Stevenson)

indigenae NOUN indigenae means natives or people from that area ❑ *an exotic that the surly indigenae will not recognise for kin* (*Wuthering Heights* by Emily Brontë)

indocible ADJ unteachable ❑ *so they were the most restive and indocible* (*Gulliver's Travels* by Jonathan Swift)

ingenuity NOUN inventiveness ❑ *entreated me to give him something as an encouragement to ingenuity* (*Gulliver's Travels* by Jonathan Swift)

ingots NOUN an ingot is a lump of a valuable metal like gold, usually shaped like a brick ❑ *Tom called the hogs "ingots"* (*The Adventures of Huckleberry Finn* by Mark Twain)

inkstand NOUN an inkstand is a pot which was put on a desk to contain either ink or pencils and pens ❑ *throwing an inkstand at the Lizard as she spoke* (*Alice's Adventures in Wonderland* by Lewis Carroll)

inordinate ADJ without order. To-day inordinate means "excessive". ❑ *Though yet untutored and inordinate* (*The Prelude* by William Wordsworth)

intellectuals NOUN here intellectuals means the minds (of the workmen) ❑ *those instructions they give being too refined for the intellectuals of their workmen* (*Gulliver's Travels* by Jonathan Swift)

interview NOUN meeting ❑ *By our first strange and fatal interview* (*On His Mistress* by John Donne)

jacks NOUN jacks are rods for turning a spit over a fire ❑ *It was a small bit of pork suspended from the kettle hanger by a string passed through a large door key, in a way known to primitive housekeepers unpossessed of jacks* (*Silas Marner* by George Eliot)

jews-harp NOUN a jews-harp is a small, metal, musical instrument that is played by the mouth ❑ *A jews-harp's plenty good enough for a rat* (*The Adventures of Huckleberry Finn* by Mark Twain)

jorum NOUN a large bowl ❑ *while Miss Skiffins brewed such a jorum of tea, that the pig in the back premises became strongly excited* (*Great Expectations* by Charles Dickens)

jostled VERB jostled means bumped or pushed by someone or some people ❑ *being jostled himself into the kennel* (*Gulliver's Travels* by Jonathan Swift)

keepsake NOUN a keepsake is a gift which reminds someone of an event or of the person who gave it to them. ❑ *books and ornaments they had in their boudoirs at home: keepsakes that different relations had presented to them* (*Jane Eyre* by Charlotte Brontë)

kenned VERB kenned means knew ❑ *though little kenned the lamplighter that he had any company but Christmas!* (*A Christmas Carol* by Charles Dickens)

kennel NOUN kennel means gutter, which is the edge of a road next to the pavement, where rain water collects and flows away ❑ *being jostled himself into the kennel* (*Gulliver's Travels* by Jonathan Swift)

knock-knee ADJ knock-knee means slanted, at an angle. ❑ *LOT 1 was marked in whitewashed knock-knee letters on the brewhouse* (*Great Expectations* by Charles Dickens)

ladylike ADJ to be ladylike is to behave in a polite, dignified and graceful way ❑ *No, winking isn't ladylike* (*Little Women* by Louisa May Alcott)

lapse NOUN flow ❑ *Stealing with silent lapse to join the brook* (*The Prelude* by William Wordsworth)

larry NOUN larry is an old word which means commotion or noisy celebration ❑ *That was all a part of the larry!* (*Tess of the D'Urbervilles* by Thomas Hardy)

laths NOUN laths are strips of wood ❑ *The panels shrunk, the windows cracked; fragments of plaster fell out of the ceiling, and the naked laths were shown instead* (*A Christmas Carol* by Charles Dickens)

leer NOUN a leer is an unpleasant smile ❑ *with a kind of leer* (*Treasure Island* by Robert Louis Stevenson)

lenitives NOUN these are different kinds of drugs or medicines: lenitives and palliatives were pain relievers; aperitives were laxatives; abstersives caused vomiting; corrosives destroyed human tissue; restringents caused constipation; cephalalgics caused headaches; icterics were used as medicine for jaundice; apophlegmatics were cough medicine, and acoustics were cures for the loss of hearing ❑ *lenitives, aperitives, abstersives, corrosives, restringents, palliatives, laxatives, cephalalgics, icterics, apophlegmatics, acoustics (Gulliver's Travels* by Jonathan Swift)

lest CONJ in case. If you do something lest something (usually) unpleasant happens you do it to try to prevent it happening ❑ *She went in without knocking, and hurried upstairs, in great fear lest she should meet the real Mary Ann (Alice's Adventures in Wonderland* by Lewis Carroll)

levee NOUN a levee is an old term for a meeting held in the morning, shortly after the person holding the meeting has got out of bed ❑ *I used to attend the King's levee once or twice a week (Gulliver's Travels* by Jonathan Swift)

life-preserver NOUN a club which had lead inside it to make it heavier and therefore more dangerous ❑ *and with no more suspicious articles displayed to view than two or three heavy bludgeons which stood in a corner, and a "life-preserver" that hung over the chimney-piece. (Oliver Twist* by Charles Dickens)

lighterman NOUN a lighterman is another word for sailor ❑ *in and out, hammers going in ship-builders' yards, saws going at timber, clashing engines going at things unknown, pumps going in leaky ships, capstans going, ships going out to sea, and unintelligible sea creatures roaring curses over the bulwarks at respondent lightermen (Great Expectations* by Charles Dickens)

livery NOUN servants often wore a uniform known as a livery ❑ *suddenly a footman in livery came running out of the wood (Alice's Adventures in Wonderland* by Lewis Carroll)

livid ADJ livid means pale or ash coloured. Livid also means very angry ❑ *a dirty, livid white (Treasure Island* by Robert Louis Stevenson)

lottery-tickets NOUN a popular card game ❑ *and Mrs. Philips protested that they would have a nice comfortable noisy game of lottery tickets (Pride and Prejudice* by Jane Austen)

lower and upper world PHRASE the earth and the heavens are the lower and upper worlds ❑ *the changes in the lower and upper world (Gulliver's Travels* by Jonathan Swift)

lustres NOUN lustres are chandeliers. A chandelier is a large, decorative frame which holds light bulbs or candles and hangs from the ceiling ❑ *the lustres, lights, the carving and the guilding (The Prelude* by William Wordsworth)

lynched VERB killed without a criminal trial by a crowd of people ❑ *He'll never know how nigh he come to getting lynched (The Adventures of Huckleberry Finn* by Mark Twain)

malingering VERB if someone is malingering they are pretending to be ill to avoid working ❑ *And you stand there malingering (Treasure Island* by Robert Louis Stevenson)

managing PHRASE treating with consideration ❑ *to think the honour of my own kind not worth managing (Gulliver's Travels* by Jonathan Swift)

manhood PHRASE manhood means human nature ❑ *concerning the nature of manhood (Gulliver's Travels* by Jonathan Swift)

man-trap NOUN a man-trap is a set of steel jaws that snap shut when trodden on and trap a person's leg

❑ *"Don't go to him,"* I called out of the window, *"he's an assassin! A man-trap!"* (Oliver Twist by Charles Dickens)

maps NOUN charts of the night sky ❑ *Let maps to others, worlds on worlds have shown* (The Good-Morrow by John Donne)

mark VERB look at or notice ❑ *Mark but this flea, and mark in this* (The Flea by John Donne)

maroons NOUN A maroon is someone who has been left in a place which it is difficult for them to escape from, like a small island ❑ *if schooners, islands, and maroons* (Treasure Island by Robert Louis Stevenson)

mast NOUN here mast means the fruit of forest trees ❑ *a quantity of acorns, dates, chestnuts, and other mast* (Gulliver's Travels by Jonathan Swift)

mate VERB defeat ❑ *Where Mars did mate the warlike Carthigens* (Doctor Faustus Chorus by Christopher Marlowe)

mealy ADJ Mealy when used to describe a face meant pallid, pale or colourless ❑ *I only know two sorts of boys. Mealy boys, and beef-faced boys* (Oliver Twist by Charles Dickens)

middling ADV fairly or moderately ❑ *she worked me middling hard for about an hour* (The Adventures of Huckleberry Finn by Mark Twain)

mill NOUN a mill, or treadmill, was a device for hard labour or punishment in prison ❑ *Was you never on the mill?* (Oliver Twist by Charles Dickens)

milliner's shop NOUN a milliner's sold fabrics, clothing, lace and accessories; as time went on they specialized more and more in hats ❑ *to pay their duty to their aunt and to a milliner's shop just over the way* (Pride and Prejudice by Jane Austen)

minching un' munching PHRASE how people in the north of England used to describe the way people

from the south speak ❑ *Minching un' munching!* (Wuthering Heights by Emily Brontë)

mine NOUN gold ❑ *Whether both th'Indias of spice and mine* (The Sun Rising by John Donne)

mire NOUN mud ❑ *Tis my fate to be always ground into the mire under the iron heel of oppression* (The Adventures of Huckleberry Finn by Mark Twain)

miscellany NOUN a miscellany is a collection of many different kinds of things ❑ *under that, the miscellany began* (Treasure Island by Robert Louis Stevenson)

mistarshers NOUN mistarshers means moustache, which is the hair that grows on a man's upper lip ❑ *when he put his hand up to his mistarshers* (Tess of the D'Urbervilles by Thomas Hardy)

morrow NOUN here good-morrow means tomorrow and a new and better life ❑ *And now good-morrow to our waking souls* (The Good-Morrow by John Donne)

mortification NOUN mortification is an old word for gangrene which is when part of the body decays or "dies" because of disease ❑ *Yes, it was a mortification–that was it* (The Adventures of Huckleberry Finn by Mark Twain)

mought VERB mought is an old spelling of might ❑ *what you mought call me? You mought call me captain* (Treasure Island by Robert Louis Stevenson)

move VERB move me not means do not make me angry ❑ *Move me not, Faustus* (Doctor Faustus 2.1 by Christopher Marlowe)

muffin-cap NOUN a muffin-cap is a flat cap made from wool ❑ *the old one, remained stationary in the muffin-cap and leathers* (Oliver Twist by Charles Dickens)

mulatter NOUN a mulatter was another word for mulatto, which is a person with parents who are from different races ❑ *a mulatter, most as white as a white man* (*The Adventures of Huckleberry Finn* by Mark Twain)

mummery NOUN mummery is an old word that meant meaningless (or pretentious) ceremony ❑ *When they were all gone, and when Trabb and his men–but not his boy: I looked for him–had crammed their mummery into bags, and were gone too, the house felt wholesomer.* (*Great Expectations* by Charles Dickens)

nap NOUN the nap is the woolly surface on a new item of clothing. Here the surface has been worn away so it looks bare ❑ *like an old hat with the nap rubbed off* (*The Adventures of Huckleberry Finn* by Mark Twain)

natural ■ NOUN a natural is a person born with learning difficulties ❑ *though he had been left to his particular care by their deceased father, who thought him almost a natural.* (*David Copperfield* by Charles Dickens) ■ ADJ natural meant illegitimate ❑ *Harriet Smith was the natural daughter of somebody* (*Emma* by Jane Austen)

navigator NOUN a navigator was originally someone employed to dig canals. It is the origin of the word "navvy" meaning a labourer ❑ *She ascertained from me in a few words what it was all about, comforted Dora, and gradually convinced her that I was not a labourer–from my manner of stating the case I believe Dora concluded that I was a navigator, and went balancing myself up and down a plank all day with a wheelbarrow–and so brought us together in peace. (David Copperfield* by Charles Dickens)·

necromancy NOUN necromancy means a kind of magic where the magician speaks to spirits or ghosts to find out what will happen in the future ❑ *He surfeits upon cursed necromancy* (*Doctor Faustus chorus* by Christopher Marlowe)

negus NOUN a negus is a hot drink made from sweetened wine and water ❑ *He sat placidly perusing the newspaper, with his little head on one side, and a glass of warm sherry negus at his elbow.* (*David Copperfield* by Charles Dickens)

nice ADJ discriminating. Able to make good judgements or choices ❑ *consequently a claim to be nice* (*Emma* by Jane Austen)

nigh ADV nigh means near ❑ *He'll never know how nigh he come to getting lynched* (*The Adventures of Huckleberry Finn* by Mark Twain)

nimbleness NOUN nimbleness means being able to move very quickly or skilfully ❑ *and with incredible accuracy and nimbleness* (*Treasure Island* by Robert Louis Stevenson)

noggin NOUN a noggin is a small mug or a wooden cup ❑ *you'll bring me one noggin of rum* (*Treasure Island* by Robert Louis Stevenson)

none ADJ neither ❑ *none can die* (*The Good-Morrow* by John Donne)

notices NOUN observations ❑ *Arch are his notices* (*The Prelude* by William Wordsworth)

occiput NOUN occiput means the back of the head ❑ *saw off the occiput of each couple* (*Gulliver's Travels* by Jonathan Swift)

officiously ADV kindly ❑ *the governess who attended Glumdalclitch very officiously lifted me up* (*Gulliver's Travels* by Jonathan Swift)

old salt PHRASE old salt is a slang term for an experienced sailor ❑ *a "true sea-dog", and a "real old salt"* (*Treasure Island* by Robert Louis Stevenson)

or ere PHRASE before ❑ *or ere the Hall was built* (*The Prelude* by William Wordsworth)

ostler NOUN one who looks after horses at an inn ❑ *The bill paid, and the waiter remembered, and the ostler not forgotten, and the chambermaid taken into consideration* (*Great Expectations* by Charles Dickens)

ostry NOUN an ostry is an old word for a pub or hotel ❑ *lest I send you into the ostry with a vengeance* (*Doctor Faustus 2.2* by Christopher Marlowe)

outrunning the constable PHRASE outrunning the constable meant spending more than you earn ❑ *but I shall by this means be able to check your bills and to pull you up if I find you outrunning the constable.* (*Great Expectations* by Charles Dickens)

over ADV across ❑ *It is in length six yards, and in the thickest part at least three yards over* (*Gulliver's Travels* by Jonathan Swift)

over the broomstick PHRASE this is a phrase meaning "getting married without a formal ceremony" ❑ *They both led tramping lives, and this woman in Gerrard-street here, had been married very young, over the broomstick (as we say), to a tramping man, and was a perfect fury in point of jealousy.* (*Great Expectations* by Charles Dickens)

own VERB own means to admit or to acknowledge ❑ *It's my old girl that advises. She has the head. But I never own to it before her. Discipline must be maintained* (*Bleak House* by Charles Dickens)

page NOUN here page means a boy employed to run errands ❑ *not my feigned page* (*On His Mistress* by John Donne)

paid pretty dear PHRASE paid pretty dear means paid a high price or suffered quite a lot ❑ *I paid pretty dear for my monthly fourpenny piece* (*Treasure Island* by Robert Louis Stevenson)

pannikins NOUN pannikins were small tin cups ❑ *of lifting light glasses and cups to his lips, as if they were clumsy pannikins* (*Great Expectations* by Charles Dickens)

pards NOUN pards are leopards ❑ *Not charioted by Bacchus and his pards* (*Ode on a Nightingale* by John Keats)

parlour boarder NOUN a pupil who lived with the family ❑ *and somebody had lately raised her from the condition of scholar to parlour boarder* (*Emma* by Jane Austen)

particular, a London PHRASE London in Victorian times and up to the 1950s was famous for having very dense fog–which was a combination of real fog and the smog of pollution from factories ❑ *This is a London particular . . . A fog, miss* (*Bleak House* by Charles Dickens)

patten NOUN pattens were wooden soles which were fixed to shoes by straps to protect the shoes in wet weather ❑ *carrying a basket like the Great Seal of England in plaited straw, a pair of pattens, a spare shawl, and an umbrella, though it was a fine bright day* (*Great Expectations* by Charles Dickens)

paviour NOUN a paviour was a labourer who worked on the street pavement ❑ *the paviour his pickaxe* (*Oliver Twist* by Charles Dickens)

peccant ADJ peccant means unhealthy ❑ *other peccant humours* (*Gulliver's Travels* by Jonathan Swift)

penetralium NOUN penetralium is a word used to describe the inner rooms of the house ❑ *and I had no desire to aggravate his impatience previous to inspecting the penetralium* (*Wuthering Heights* by Emily Brontë)

pensive ADV pensive means deep in thought or thinking seriously about something ❑ *and she was leaning pensive on a tomb-stone on her right elbow* (*The Adventures of Huckleberry Finn* by Mark Twain)

penury NOUN penury is the state of being extremely poor ❑ *Distress, if not penury, loomed in the distance* (*Tess of the D'Urbervilles* by Thomas Hardy)

perspective NOUN telescope ❑ *a pocket perspective* (*Gulliver's Travels* by Jonathan Swift)

phaeton NOUN a phaeton was an open carriage for four people ❑ *often* condescends to drive by my humble abode in her little phaeton and ponies (*Pride and Prejudice* by Jane Austen)

phantasm NOUN a phantasm is an illusion, something that is not real. It is sometimes used to mean ghost ❑ *Experience had bred no fancies in him that could raise the phantasm of appetite* (*Silas Marner* by George Eliot)

physic NOUN here physic means medicine ❑ *there I studied physic two years and seven months* (*Gulliver's Travels* by Jonathan Swift)

pinioned VERB to pinion is to hold both arms so that a person cannot move them ❑ *But the relentless Ghost pinioned him in both his arms, and forced him to observe what happened next.* (*A Christmas Carol* by Charles Dickens)

piquet NOUN piquet was a popular card game in the C18th ❑ *Mr Hurst and Mr Bingley were at piquet* (*Pride and Prejudice* by Jane Austen)

plaister NOUN a plaister is a piece of cloth on which an apothecary (or pharmacist) would spread ointment. The cloth is then applied to wounds or bruises to treat them ❑ *Then, she gave the knife a final smart wipe on the edge of the plaister, and then sawed a very thick round off the loaf: which she finally, before separating from the loaf, hewed into two halves, of which Joe got one, and I the other.* (*Great Expectations* by Charles Dickens)

plantations NOUN here plantations means colonies, which are countries controlled by a more powerful country ❑ *besides our plantations in America* (*Gulliver's Travels* by Jonathan Swift)

plastic ADJ here plastic is an old term meaning shaping or a power that was forming ❑ *A plastic power abode with me* (*The Prelude* by William Wordsworth)

players NOUN actors ❑ *of players which upon the world's stage be* (*On His Mistress* by John Donne)

plump ADV all at once, suddenly ❑ *But it took a bit of time to get it well round, the change come so uncommon plump, didn't it?* (*Great Expectations* by Charles Dickens)

plundered VERB to plunder is to rob or steal from ❑ *These crosses stand for the names of ships or towns that they sank or plundered* (*Treasure Island* by Robert Louis Stevenson)

pommel ■ VERB to pommel someone is to hit them repeatedly with your fists ❑ *hug him round the neck, pommel his back, and kick his legs in irrepressible affection!* (*A Christmas Carol* by Charles Dickens) ■ NOUN a pommel is the part of a saddle that rises up at the front ❑ *He had his gun across his pommel* (*The Adventures of Huckleberry Finn* by Mark Twain)

poor's rates NOUN poor's rates were property taxes which were used to support the poor ❑ *"Oh!" replied the undertaker; "why, you know, Mr. Bumble, I pay a good deal towards the poor's rates."* (*Oliver Twist* by Charles Dickens)

popular ADJ popular means ruled by the people, or Republican, rather than ruled by a monarch ❑ *With those of Greece compared and popular Rome* (*The Prelude* by William Wordsworth)

porringer NOUN a porringer is a small bowl ❑ *Of this festive composition each boy had one porringer, and no more* (*Oliver Twist* by Charles Dickens)

postboy NOUN a postboy was the driver of a horse-drawn carriage ❑ *He spoke to a postboy who was dozing under the gateway* (*Oliver Twist* by Charles Dickens)

post-chaise NOUN a fast carriage for two or four passengers ❑ *Looking round, he saw that it was a post-chaise, driven at great speed* (*Oliver Twist* by Charles Dickens)

postern NOUN a small gate usually at the back of a building ❑ *The little servant happening to be entering the* *fortress with two hot rolls, I passed through the postern and crossed the drawbridge, in her company* (*Great Expectations* by Charles Dickens)

pottle NOUN a pottle was a small basket ❑ *He had a paper-bag under each arm and a pottle of strawberries in one hand . . .* (*Great Expectations* by Charles Dickens)

pounce NOUN pounce is a fine powder used to prevent ink spreading on untreated paper ❑ *in that grim atmosphere of pounce and parchment, red-tape, dusty wafers, ink-jars, brief and draft paper, law reports, writs, declarations, and bills of costs* (*David Copperfield* by Charles Dickens)

pox NOUN pox means sexually transmitted diseases like syphilis ❑ *how the pox in all its consequences and denominations* (*Gulliver's Travels* by Jonathan Swift)

prelibation NOUN prelibation means a foretaste of or an example of something to come ❑ *A prelibation to the mower's scythe* (*The Prelude* by William Wordsworth)

prentice NOUN an apprentice ❑ *and Joe, sitting on an old gun, had told me that when I was 'prentice to him regularly bound, we would have such Larks there!* (*Great Expectations* by Charles Dickens)

presently ADV immediately ❑ *I presently knew what they meant* (*Gulliver's Travels* by Jonathan Swift)

pumpion NOUN pumpkin ❑ *for it was almost as large as a small pumpion* (*Gulliver's Travels* by Jonathan Swift)

punctual ADJ kept in one place ❑ *was not a punctual presence, but a spirit* (*The Prelude* by William Wordsworth)

quadrille ■ NOUN a quadrille is a dance invented in France which is usually performed by four couples ❑ *However, Mr Swiveller had Miss Sophy's hand for the first quadrille* (*country-dances being low, were utterly proscribed*) (*The Old Curiosity Shop* by Charles Dickens) ■ NOUN quadrille was a card game for four people ❑ *to make up her pool of quadrille in the evening* (*Pride and Prejudice* by Jane Austen)

quality NOUN gentry or upper-class people ❑ *if you are with the quality* (*The Adventures of Huckleberry Finn* by Mark Twain)

quick parts PHRASE quick-witted ❑ *Mr Bennet was so odd a mixture of quick parts* (*Pride and Prejudice* by Jane Austen)

quid NOUN a quid is something chewed or kept in the mouth, like a piece of tobacco ❑ *rolling his quid* (*Treasure Island* by Robert Louis Stevenson)

quit VERB quit means to avenge or to make even ❑ *But Faustus's death shall quit my infamy* (*Doctor Faustus 4.3* by Christopher Marlowe)

rags NOUN divisions ❑ *Nor hours, days, months, which are the rags of time* (*The Sun Rising* by John Donne)

raiment NOUN raiment means clothing ❑ *the mountain shook off turf and flower, had only heath for raiment and crag for gem* (*Jane Eyre* by Charlotte Brontë)

rain cats and dogs PHRASE an expression meaning rain heavily. The origin of the expression is unclear ❑ *But it'll perhaps rain cats and dogs to-morrow* (*Silas Marner* by George Eliot)

raised Cain PHRASE raised Cain means caused a lot of trouble. Cain is a character in the Bible who killed his brother Abel ❑ *and every time he got drunk he raised Cain around town* (*The Adventures of Huckleberry Finn* by Mark Twain)

rambling ADJ rambling means confused and not very clear ❑ *my head began to be filled very early with rambling thoughts* (*Robinson Crusoe* by Daniel Defoe)

raree-show NOUN a raree-show is an old term for a peep-show or a fairground entertainment ❏ *A raree-show is here, with children gathered round* (*The Prelude* by William Wordsworth)

recusants NOUN people who resisted authority ❏ *hardy recusants* (*The Prelude* by William Wordsworth)

redounding VERB eddying. An eddy is a movement in water or air which goes round and round instead of flowing in one direction ❏ *mists and steam-like fogs redounding everywhere* (*The Prelude* by William Wordsworth)

redundant ADJ here redundant means overflowing but Wordsworth also uses it to mean excessively large or too big ❏ *A tempest, a redundant energy* (*The Prelude* by William Wordsworth)

reflex NOUN reflex is a shortened version of reflexion, which is an alternative spelling of reflection ❏ *To cut across the reflex of a star* (*The Prelude* by William Wordsworth)

Reformatory NOUN a prison for young offenders/criminals ❏ *Even when I was taken to have a new suit of clothes, the tailor had orders to make them like a kind of Reformatory, and on no account to let me have the free use of my limbs.* (*Great Expectations* by Charles Dickens)

remorse NOUN pity or compassion ❏ *by that remorse* (*On His Mistress* by John Donne)

render VERB in this context render means give. ❏ *and Sarah could render no reason that would be sanctioned by the feeling of the community.* (*Silas Marner* by George Eliot)

repeater NOUN a repeater was a watch that chimed the last hour when a button was pressed—as a result it was useful in the dark ❏ *And his watch is a gold repeater, and worth a hundred pound if it's worth a*

penny. (*Great Expectations* by Charles Dickens)

repugnance NOUN repugnance means a strong dislike of something or someone ❏ *overcoming a strong repugnance* (*Treasure Island* by Robert Louis Stevenson)

reverence NOUN reverence means bow. When you bow to someone, you briefly bend your body towards them as a formal way of showing them respect ❏ *made my reverence* (*Gulliver's Travels* by Jonathan Swift)

reverie NOUN a reverie is a daydream ❏ *I can guess the subject of your reverie* (*Pride and Prejudice* by Jane Austen)

revival NOUN a religious meeting held in public ❏ *well I'd ben a-running' a little temperance revival thar' bout a week* (*The Adventures of Huckleberry Finn* by Mark Twain)

revolt VERB revolt means turn back or stop your present course of action and go back to what you were doing before ❏ *Revolt, or I'll in piecemeal tear thy flesh* (*Doctor Faustus* 5.1 by Christopher Marlowe)

rheumatics/rheumatism NOUN rheumatics [rheumatism] is an illness that makes your joints or muscles stiff and painful ❏ *a new cure for the rheumatics* (*Treasure Island* by Robert Louis Stevenson)

riddance NOUN riddance is usually used in the form good riddance which you say when you are pleased that something has gone or been left behind ❏ *I'd better go into the house, and die and be a riddance* (*David Copperfield* by Charles Dickens)

rimy ADJ rimy is an adjective which means covered in ice or frost ❏ *It was a rimy morning, and very damp* (*Great Expectations* by Charles Dickens)

riper ADJ riper means more mature or older ❏ *At riper years to Wittenberg he went* (*Doctor Faustus* chorus by Christopher Marlowe)

rubber NOUN a set of games in whist or backgammon ❑ *her father was sure of his rubber* (*Emma* by Jane Austen)

ruffian NOUN a ruffian is a person who behaves violently ❑ *and when the ruffian had told him* (*Treasure Island* by Robert Louis Stevenson)

sadness NOUN sadness is an old term meaning seriousness ❑ *But I prithee tell me, in good sadness* (*Doctor Faustus 2.2* by Christopher Marlowe)

sailed before the mast PHRASE this phrase meant someone who did not look like a sailor ❑ *he had none of the appearance of a man that sailed before the mast* (*Treasure Island* by Robert Louis Stevenson)

scabbard NOUN a scabbard is the covering for a sword or dagger ❑ *Girded round its middle was an antique scabbard; but no sword was in it, and the ancient sheath was eaten up with rust* (*A Christmas Carol* by Charles Dickens)

schooners NOUN A schooner is a fast, medium-sized sailing ship ❑ *if schooners, islands, and maroons* (*Treasure Island* by Robert Louis Stevenson)

science NOUN learning or knowledge ❑ *Even Sciencè, too, at hand* (*The Prelude* by William Wordsworth)

scrouge VERB to scrouge means to squeeze or to crowd ❑ *to scrouge in and get a sight* (*The Adventures of Huckleberry Finn* by Mark Twain)

scrutore NOUN a scrutore, or escritoire, was a writing table ❑ *set me gently on my feet upon the scrutore* (*Gulliver's Travels* by Jonathan Swift)

scutcheon/escutcheon NOUN an escutcheon is a shield with a coat of arms, or the symbols of a family name, engraved on it ❑ *On the scutcheon we'll have a bend* (*The Adventures of Huckleberry Finn* by Mark Twain)

sea-dog PHRASE sea-dog is a slang term for an experienced sailor or pirate ❑ *a "true sea-dog", and a "real old salt,"* (*Treasure Island* by Robert Louis Stevenson)

see the lions PHRASE to see the lions was to go and see the sights of London. Originally the phrase referred to the menagerie in the Tower of London and later in Regent's Park ❑ *We will go and see the lions for an hour or two–it's something to have a fresh fellow like you to show them to,* Copperfield (*David Copperfield* by Charles Dickens)

self-conceit NOUN self-conceit is an old term which means having too high an opinion of oneself, or deceiving yourself ❑ *Till swollen with cunning, of a self-conceit* (*Doctor Faustus chorus* by Christopher Marlowe)

seneschal NOUN a steward ❑ *where a grey-headed seneschal sings a funny chorus with a funnier body of vassals* (*Oliver Twist* by Charles Dickens)

sensible ADJ if you were sensible of something you are aware or conscious of something ❑ *If my children are silly I must hope to be always sensible of it* (*Pride and Prejudice* by Jane Austen)

sessions NOUN court cases were heard at specific times of the year called sessions ❑ *He lay in prison very ill, during the whole interval between his committal for trial, and the coming round of the Sessions.* (*Great Expectations* by Charles Dickens)

shabby ADJ shabby places look old and in bad condition ❑ *a little bit of a shabby village named Pikesville* (*The Adventures of Huckleberry Finn* by Mark Twain)

shay-cart NOUN a shay-cart was a small cart drawn by one horse ❑ *"I were at the Bargemen t'other night, Pip;" whenever he subsided into affection, he called me Pip, and whenever he relapsed into politeness he called me Sir; "when there come up in his* *shay-cart Pumblechook."* (*Great Expectations* by Charles Dickens)

shilling NOUN a shilling is an old unit of currency. There were twenty shillings in every British pound ❑ *"Ten shillings too much," said the gentleman in the white waistcoat.* (*Oliver Twist* by Charles Dickens)

shines NOUN tricks or games ❑ *well, it would make a cow laugh to see the shines that old idiot cut* (*The Adventures of Huckleberry Finn* by Mark Twain)

shirking VERB shirking means not doing what you are meant to be doing, or evading your duties ❑ *some of you shirking lubbers* (*Treasure Island* by Robert Louis Stevenson)

shiver my timbers PHRASE shiver my timbers is an expression which was used by sailors and pirates to express surprise ❑ *why, shiver my timbers, if I hadn't forgotten my score!* (*Treasure Island* by Robert Louis Stevenson)

shoe-roses NOUN shoe-roses were roses made from ribbons which were stuck on to shoes as decoration ❑ *the very shoe-roses for Netherfield were got by proxy* (*Pride and Prejudice* by Jane Austen)

singular ADJ singular means very great and remarkable or strange ❑ *"Singular dream," he says* (*The Adventures of Huckleberry Finn* by Mark Twain)

sire NOUN sire is an old word which means lord or master or elder ❑ *She also defied her sire* (*Little Women* by Louisa May Alcott)

sixpence NOUN a sixpence was half of a shilling ❑ *if she had only a shilling in the world, she would be very lilkely to give away sixpence of it* (*Emma* by Jane Austen)

slavey NOUN the word slavey was used when there was only one servant in a house or boarding-house–so she had to perform all the duties of a larger staff ❑ *Two distinct knocks, sir, will produce the slavey at any*

time (*The Old Curiosity Shop* by Charles Dickens)

slender ADJ weak ❑ *In slender accents of sweet verse* (*The Prelude* by William Wordsworth)

slop-shops NOUN slop-shops were shops where cheap ready-made clothes were sold. They mainly sold clothes to sailors ❑ *Accordingly, I took the jacket off, that I might learn to do without it; and carrying it under my arm, began a tour of inspection of the various slop-shops.* (*David Copperfield* by Charles Dickens)

sluggard NOUN a lazy person ❑ *"Stand up and repeat ''Tis the voice of the sluggard,'" said the Gryphon.* (*Alice's Adventures in Wonderland* by Lewis Carroll)

smallpox NOUN smallpox is a serious infectious disease ❑ *by telling the men we had smallpox aboard* (*The Adventures of Huckleberry Finn* by Mark Twain)

smalls NOUN smalls are short trousers ❑ *It is difficult for a large-headed, small-eyed youth, of lumbering make and heavy countenance, to look dignified under any circumstances; but it is more especially so, when superadded to these personal attractions are a red nose and yellow smalls* (*Oliver Twist* by Charles Dickens)

sneeze-box NOUN a box for snuff was called a sneeze-box because sniffing snuff makes the user sneeze ❑ *To think of Jack Dawkins–lummy Jack –the Dodger–the Artful Dodger– going abroad for a common twopen-ny-halfpenny sneeze-box!* (*Oliver Twist* by Charles Dickens)

snorted VERB slept ❑ *Or snorted we in the Seven Sleepers' den?* (*The Good-Morrow* by John Donne)

snuff NOUN snuff is tobacco in powder form which is taken by sniffing ❑ *as he thrust his thumb and fore-finger into the proffered snuff-box of the undertaker: which was an ingenious little model of a patent* coffin. (*Oliver Twist* by Charles Dickens)

soliloquized VERB to soliloquize is when an actor in a play speaks to himself or herself rather than to another actor ❏ *"A new servitude! There is something in that," I soliloquized (mentally, be it understood; I did not talk aloud)* (*Jane Eyre* by Charlotte Brontë)

sough NOUN a sough is a drain or a ditch ❏ *as you may have noticed the sough that runs from the marshes* (*Wuthering Heights* by Emily Brontë)

spirits NOUN a spirit is the nonphysical part of a person which is believed to remain alive after their death ❏ *that I might raise up spirits when I please* (*Doctor Faustus* 1.5 by Christopher Marlowe)

spleen ■ NOUN here spleen means a type of sadness or depression which was thought to only affect the wealthy ❏ *yet here I could plainly discover the true seeds of spleen* (*Gulliver's Travels* by Jonathan Swift) ■ NOUN irritability and low spirits ❏ *Adieu to disappointment and spleen* (*Pride and Prejudice* by Jane Austen)

spondulicks NOUN spondulicks is a slang word which means money ❏ *not for all his spondulicks and as much more on top of it* (*The Adventures of Huckleberry Finn* by Mark Twain)

stalled of VERB to be stalled of something is to be bored with it ❏ *I'm stalled of doing naught* (*Wuthering Heights* by Emily Brontë)

stanchion NOUN a stanchion is a pole or bar that stands upright and is used as a building support ❏ *and slid down a stanchion* (*The Adventures of Huckleberry Finn* by Mark Twain)

stang NOUN stang is another word for pole which was an old measurement ❏ *These fields were intermingled with woods of half a stang* (*Gulliver's Travels* by Jonathan Swift)

starlings NOUN a starling is a wall built around the pillars that support a bridge to protect the pillars ❏ *There were states of the tide when, having been down the river, I could not get back through the eddy-chafed arches and starlings of old London Bridge* (*Great Expectations* by Charles Dickens)

startings NOUN twitching or night-time movements of the body ❏ *with midnight's startings* (*On His Mistress* by John Donne)

stomacher NOUN a panel at the front of a dress ❏ *but send her aunt the pattern of a stomacher* (*Emma* by Jane Austen)

stoop VERB swoop ❏ *Once a kite hovering over the garden made a stoop at me* (*Gulliver's Travels* by Jonathan Swift)

succedaneum NOUN a succedaneum is a substitute ❏ *But as a succedaneum* (*The Prelude* by William Wordsworth)

suet NOUN a hard animal fat used in cooking ❏ *and your jaws are too weak For anything tougher than suet* (*Alice's Adventures in Wonderland* by Lewis Carroll)

sultry ADJ sultry weather is hot and damp. Here sultry means unpleasant or risky ❏ *for it was getting pretty sultry for us* (*The Adventures of Huckleberry Finn* by Mark Twain)

summerset NOUN summerset is an old spelling of somersault. If someone does a somersault, they turn over completely in the air ❏ *I have seen him do the summerset* (*Gulliver's Travels* by Jonathan Swift)

supper NOUN supper was a light meal taken late in the evening. The main meal was dinner which was eaten at four or five in the afternoon ❏ *and the supper table was all set out* (*Emma* by Jane Austen)

surfeits VERB to surfeit in something is to have far too much of it, or to overindulge in it to an unhealthy degree ❏ *He surfeits upon cursed* *necromancy* (*Doctor Faustus chorus* by Christopher Marlowe)

surtout NOUN a surtout is a long close-fitting overcoat ❑ *He wore a long black surtout reaching nearly to his ankles* (*The Old Curiosity Shop* by Charles Dickens)

swath NOUN swath is the width of corn cut by a scythe ❑ *while thy hook Spares the next swath* (*Ode to Autumn* by John Keats)

sylvan ADJ sylvan means belonging to the woods ❑ *Sylvan historian* (*Ode on a Grecian Urn* by John Keats)

taction NOUN taction means touch. This means that the people had to be touched on the mouth or the ears to get their attention ❑ *without being roused by some external taction upon the organs of speech and hearing* (*Gulliver's Travels* by Jonathan Swift)

Tag and Rag and Bobtail PHRASE the riff-raff, or lower classes. Used in an insulting way ❑ *"No," said he; "not till it got about that there was no protection on the premises, and it come to be considered dangerous, with convicts and Tag and Rag and Bobtail going up and down."* (*Great Expectations* by Charles Dickens)

tallow NOUN tallow is hard animal fat that is used to make candles and soap ❑ *and a lot of tallow candles* (*The Adventures of Huckleberry Finn* by Mark Twain)

tan VERB to tan means to beat or whip ❑ *and if I catch you about that school I'll tan you good* (*The Adventures of Huckleberry Finn* by Mark Twain)

tanyard NOUN the tanyard is part of a tannery, which is a place where leather is made from animal skins ❑ *hid in the old tanyard* (*The Adventures of Huckleberry Finn* by Mark Twain)

tarry ADJ tarry means the colour of tar or black ❑ *his tarry pig-tail*

(*Treasure Island* by Robert Louis Stevenson)

thereof PHRASE from there ❑ *By all desires which thereof did ensue* (*On His Mistress* by John Donne)

thick with, be PHRASE if you are "thick with someone" you are very close, sharing secrets–it is often used to describe people who are planning something secret ❑ *Hasn't he been thick with Mr Heathcliff lately?* (*Wuthering Heights* by Emily Brontë)

thimble NOUN a thimble is a small cover used to protect the finger while sewing ❑ *The paper had been sealed in several places by a thimble* (*Treasure Island* by Robert Louis Stevenson)

thirtover ADJ thirtover is an old word which means obstinate or that someone is very determined to do want they want and can not be persuaded to do something in another way ❑ *I have been living on in a thirtover, lackadaisical way* (*Tess of the D'Urbervilles* by Thomas Hardy)

timbrel NOUN timbrel is a tambourine ❑ *What pipes and timbrels?* (*Ode on a Grecian Urn* by John Keats)

tin NOUN tin is slang for money/cash ❑ *Then the plain question is, an't it a pity that this state of things should continue, and how much better would it be for the old gentleman to hand over a reasonable amount of tin, and make it all right and comfortable* (*The Old Curiosity Shop* by Charles Dickens)

tincture NOUN a tincture is a medicine made with alcohol and a small amount of a drug ❑ *with ink composed of a cephalic tincture* (*Gulliver's Travels* by Jonathan Swift)

tithe NOUN a tithe is a tax paid to the church ❑ *and held farms which, speaking from a spiritual point of view, paid highly-desirable tithes* (*Silas Marner* by George Eliot)

towardly ADJ a towardly child is dutiful or obedient ❏ *and a towardly child* (*Gulliver's Travels* by Jonathan Swift)

toys NOUN trifles are things which are considered to have little importance, value, or significance ❏ *purchase my life from them bysome bracelets, glass rings, and other toys* (*Gulliver's Travels* by Jonathan Swift)

tract NOUN a tract is a religious pamphlet or leaflet ❏ *and Joe Harper got a hymn-book and a tract* (*The Adventures of Huckleberry Finn* by Mark Twain)

train-oil NOUN train-oil is oil from whale blubber ❏ *The train-oil and gunpowder were shoved out of sight in a minute* (*Wuthering Heights* by Emily Brontë)

tribulation NOUN tribulation means the suffering or difficulty you experience in a particular situation ❏ *Amy was learning this distinction through much tribulation* (*Little Women* by Louisa May Alcott)

trivet NOUN a trivet is a three-legged stand for resting a pot or kettle ❏ *a pocket-knife in his right; and a pewter pot on the trivet* (*Oliver Twist* by Charles Dickens)

trot line NOUN a trot line is a fishing line to which a row of smaller fishing lines are attached ❏ *when he got along I was hard at it taking up a trot line* (*The Adventures of Huckleberry Finn* by Mark Twain)

troth NOUN oath or pledge ❏ *I wonder, by my troth* (*The Good-Morrow* by John Donne)

truckle NOUN a truckle bedstead is a bed that is on wheels and can be slid under another bed to save space ❏ *It rose under my hand, and the door yielded. Looking in, I saw a lighted candle on a table, a bench, and a mattress on a truckle bedstead.* (*Great Expectations* by Charles Dickens)

trump NOUN a trump is a good, reliable person who can be trusted ❏ *This lad Hawkins is a trump, I perceive* (*Treasure Island* by Robert Louis Stevenson)

tucker NOUN a tucker is a frilly lace collar which is worn around the neck ❏ *Whereat Scrooge's niece's sister—the plump one with the lace tucker: not the one with the roses—blushed.* (*A Christmas Carol* by Charles Dickens)

tureen NOUN a large bowl with a lid from which soup or vegetables are served ❏ *Waiting in a hot tureen!* (*Alice's Adventures in Wonderland* by Lewis Carroll)

turnkey NOUN a prison officer; jailer ❏ *As we came out of the prison through the lodge, I found that the great importance of my guardian was appreciated by the turnkeys, no less than by those whom they held in charge.* (*Great Expectations* by Charles Dickens)

turnpike NOUN the upkeep of many roads of the time was paid for by tolls (fees) collected at posts along the road. There was a gate to prevent people travelling further along the road until the toll had been paid. ❏. *Traddles, whom I have taken up by appointment at the turnpike, presents a dazzling combination of cream colour and light blue; and both he and Mr. Dick have a general effect about them of being all gloves.* (*David Copperfield* by Charles Dickens)

twas PHRASE it was ❏ *twas but a dream of thee* (*The Good-Morrow* by John Donne)

tyrannized VERB tyrannized means bullied or forced to do things against their will ❏ *for people would soon cease coming there to be tyrannized over and put down* (*Treasure Island* by Robert Louis Stevenson)

'un NOUN 'un is a slang term for one—usually used to refer to a person ❏ *She's been thinking the old 'un* (*David Copperfield* by Charles Dickens)

undistinguished ADJ undiscriminating or incapable of making a distinction between good and bad things ❏

their undistinguished appetite to devour everything (*Gulliver's Travels* by Jonathan Swift)

use NOUN habit ❏ *Though use make you apt to kill me* (*The Flea* by John Donne)

vacant ADJ vacant usually means empty, but here Wordsworth uses it to mean carefree ❏ *To vacant musing, unreproved neglect* (*The Prelude* by William Wordsworth)

valetudinarian NOUN one too concerned with his or her own health. ❏ *for having been a valetudinarian all his life* (*Emma* by Jane Austen)

vamp VERB vamp means to walk or tramp to somewhere ❏ *Well, vamp on to Marlott, will 'ee* (*Tess of the D'Urbervilles* by Thomas Hardy)

vapours NOUN the vapours is an old term which means unpleasant and strange thoughts, which make the person feel nervous and unhappy ❏ *and my head was full of vapours* (*Robinson Crusoe* by Daniel Defoe)

vegetables NOUN here vegetables means plants ❏ *the other vegetables are in the same proportion* (*Gulliver's Travels* by Jonathan Swift)

venturesome ADJ if you are venturesome you are willing to take risks ❏ *he must be either hopelessly stupid or a venturesome fool* (*Wuthering Heights* by Emily Brontë)

verily ADV verily means really or truly ❏ *though I believe verily* (*Robinson Crusoe* by Daniel Defoe)

vicinage NOUN vicinage is an area or the residents of an area ❏ *and to his thought the whole vicinage was haunted by her.* (*Silas Marner* by George Eliot)

victuals NOUN victuals means food ❏ *grumble a little over the victuals* (*The Adventures of Huckleberry Finn* by Mark Twain)

vintage NOUN vintage in this context means wine ❏ *Oh, for a draught of*

vintage! (*Ode on a Nightingale* by John Keats)

virtual ADJ here virtual means powerful or strong ❏ *had virtual faith* (*The Prelude* by William Wordsworth)

vittles NOUN vittles is a slang word which means food ❏ *There never was such a woman for givin' away vittles and drink* (*Little Women* by Louisa May Alcott)

voided straight PHRASE voided straight is an old expression which means emptied immediately ❏ *see the rooms be voided straight* (*Doctor Faustus* 4.1 by Christopher Marlowe)

wainscot NOUN wainscot is wood panel lining in a room so wainscoted means a room lined with wooden panels ❏ *in the dark wainscoted parlor* (*Silas Marner* by George Eliot)

walking the plank PHRASE walking the plank was a punishment in which a prisoner would be made to walk along a plank on the side of the ship and fall into the sea, where they would be abandoned ❏ *about hanging, and walking the plank* (*Treasure Island* by Robert Louis Stevenson)

want VERB want means to be lacking or short of ❏ *The next thing wanted was to get the picture framed* (*Emma* by Jane Austen)

wanting ADJ wanting means lacking or missing ❏ *wanting two fingers of the left hand* (*Treasure Island* by Robert Louis Stevenson)

wanting, I was not PHRASE I was not wanting means I did not fail ❏ *I was not wanting to lay a foundation of religious knowledge in his mind* (*Robinson Crusoe* by Daniel Defoe)

ward NOUN a ward is, usually, a child who has been put under the protection of the court or a guardian for his or her protection ❏ *I call the Wards in Jarndyce. They* *are caged up with all the others. (Bleak House* by Charles Dickens)

waylay VERB to waylay someone is to lie in wait for them or to intercept them ❑ *I must go up the road and waylay him (The Adventures of Huckleberry Finn* by Mark Twain)

weazen NOUN weazen is a slang word for throat. It actually means shrivelled ❑ *You with a uncle too! Why, I knowed you at Gargery's when you was so small a wolf that I could have took your weazen betwixt this finger and thumb and chucked you away dead (Great Expectations* by Charles Dickens)

wery ■ ADV very ❑ *Be wery careful o' vidders all your life (Pickwick Papers* by Charles Dickens) ■ *See* wibrated

wherry NOUN wherry is a small swift rowing boat for one person ❑ *It was flood tide when Daniel Quilp sat himself down in the wherry to cross to the opposite shore. (The Old Curiosity Shop* by Charles Dickens)

whether PREP whether means which of the two in this example ❑ *we came in full view of a great island or continent (for we knew not whether) (Gulliver's Travels* by Jonathan Swift)

whetstone NOUN a whetstone is a stone used to sharpen knives and other tools ❑ *I dropped pap's whetstone there too (The Adventures of Huckleberry Finn* by Mark Twain)

wibrated VERB in Dickens's use of the English language "w" often replaces "v" when he is reporting speech. So here "wibrated" means "vibrated". In *Pickwick Papers* a judge asks Sam Weller (who constantly confuses the two letters) "Do you spell it with a 'v' or a 'w'?" to which Weller replies "That depends upon the taste and fancy of the speller, my Lord" ❑ *There are strings . . . in the human heart that had better not be wibrated (Barnaby Rudge* by Charles Dickens)

wicket NOUN a wicket is a little door in a larger entrance ❑ *Having rested here, for a minute or so, to collect a good burst of sobs and an imposing show of tears and terror, he knocked loudly at the wicket (Oliver Twist* by Charles Dickens)

without CONJ without means unless ❑ *You don't know about me, without you have read a book by the name of The Adventures of Tom Sawyer (The Adventures of Huckleberry Finn* by Mark Twain)

wittles ■ NOUN wittles is a slang word which means food ❑ *I live on broken wittles—and I sleep on the coals (David Copperfield* by Charles Dickens) ■ *See* wibrated

woo VERB courts or forms a proper relationship with ❑ *before it woo (The Flea* by John Donne)

words, to have PHRASE if you have words with someone you have a disagreement or an argument ❑ *I do not want to have words with a young thing like you. (Black Beauty* by Anna Sewell)

workhouse NOUN workhouses were places where the homeless were given food and a place to live in return for doing very hard work ❑ *And the Union workhouses? demanded Scrooge. Are they still in operation? (A Christmas Carol* by Charles Dickens)

yawl NOUN a yawl is a small boat kept on a bigger boat for short trips. Yawl is also the name for a small fishing boat ❑ *She sent out her yawl, and we went aboard (The Adventures of Huckleberry Finn* by Mark Twain)

yeomanry NOUN the yeomanry was a collective term for the middle classes involved in agriculture ❑ *The yeomanry are precisely the order of people with whom I feel I can have nothing to do (Emma* by Jane Austen)

yonder ADV yonder means over there ❑ *all in the same second we seem to hear low voices in yonder! (The Adventures of Huckleberry Finn* by Mark Twain)